THE MOON HORSE

THE MOON HORSE

A NOVEL

TANYA KERN

SUNSTONE
PRESS

SANTA FE

Sunstone books may be purchased for educational, business, or sales promotional use.
For information please write: Special Markets Department, Sunstone Press,
P.O. Box 2321, Santa Fe, New Mexico 87504-2321.

Book and cover design › R. Ahl
Printed on acid-free paper
∞
eBook 978-1-61139-682-9

Library of Congress Cataloging-in-Publication Data

Names: Kern, Tanya, 1959- author.
Title: The moon horse : a novel / by Tanya Kern.
Description: Santa Fe, NM : Sunstone Press, [2022] | Summary: "Toni, a
  young woman looking for love and happiness during the drug and alcohol
  infested era of the 1990s has to save her own life as well as the life
  of her beautiful horse"-- Provided by publisher.
Identifiers: LCCN 2022019578 | ISBN 9781632933577 (paperback) | ISBN
  9781611396829 (epub)
Subjects: LCGFT: Novels.
Classification: LCC PS3611.E757 M66 2022 | DDC 813/.6--dc23/eng/20220513
LC record available at https://lccn.loc.gov/2022019578

WWW.SUNSTONEPRESS.COM
SUNSTONE PRESS / POST OFFICE BOX 2321 / SANTA FE, NM 87504-2321 /USA
(505) 988-4418 / FAX (505) 988-1025

PREFACE

The story of The Moon Horse is very close to my heart. I ask myself, "Why do bad accidents happen to good people? Why are jewels abused?" It doesn't make sense to me. There is no explanation for it. I force myself to focus on another question: "How can this damage be healed?"

In the conventional world we live in, doctors, lawyers, therapists, judges and veterinarians are our authority figures. When they tell us that our loved ones will not make it, we feel hopeless. When they tell us that we won't survive, we feel helpless.

I was raised by nonconformist parents in a counter-culture world. Both my parents were free thinkers. My mother was a very strong woman who taught me, by her example, that a woman can navigate her life, have adventures on her own and be a heroine. My mother believed that a woman doesn't need to wait around for Prince Charming to live a fairy tale of her own making. My mother raised me on organic foods when all my peers at my public elementary school were eating white bread, bologna and American cheese sandwiches. My father believed in intentional poverty and living off the land in a house that one built by oneself in a time when people sacrificed their lives to work at a nine to five job they disliked so they could make money to buy a big house in a suburban neighborhood. My parents went against the flow of the society of their generation. They were called beatniks and then hippies. I am their flower child.

My parents believed in alternative healing. For them, Mother Nature was the best cure. My mother always told me that with time and patience, Mother Nature could work miracles. My parents did not listen to the hopeless and helpless verdicts of the authority figures.

What I love about the counter-culture movement is that people were encouraged to express their feelings. They were allowed to be individuals and sovereigns of their own lives. There was no ruler or authority figure that could dictate to them how they should live, what they should do or how they should think. Individuality was sacred. Originality and creativity was worshipped. In this culture, I thrived.

I learned to think, feel and see things for myself. Yes, I was vulnerable and I often was fooled by people who tried to manipulate me. I am an innocent. I am pure emotion. And my life partners are the innocent and emotional creatures of Mother Earth. The bond that I share with animals is both deep-seated and divine. I believe that animals have both feelings and souls.

To me, the Arabian horse is the most majestic. Arabian horses are royalty. A Bedouin story states that Allah created the Arabian horse from the four winds; spirit from the North, strength from the South, speed from the East and intelligence from the West. Allah exclaimed, "I establish thee as one of the glories of the Earth. I give thee flight without wings. I have hung happiness from the forelock which hangs between your eyes. You shall be the Lord of the other animals. Men shall follow you wherever you go. Riches shall be on your back and fortune shall come through your meditation."

Every day, I pray to find the purpose for my life with the courage to achieve it. If my only purpose is to try to save an Arabian horse's life or to try to save myself, then I am grateful for my determination to heal and repair the harm.

THE MOON HORSE

It's the Fourth of July. The day of freedom. I am determined to find an isolated Hispanic village sixty miles south of my ranch where there is a young gray Arabian horse that I want to buy. Pearce, my boyfriend, is sitting in the passenger side of my small pickup truck, complaining that we are already lost. I am driving my little blue truck through miles of dirt roads that seem to lead us nowhere.

"Just turn around and go home, Toni. You don't need to look at another horse anyway," Pearce says impatiently. I know Pearce is against me buying another horse.

"But Silvano is lonely. I know that horses are social creatures. I can't bear to think of Silvano secluded by himself in his corral every day," I say firmly. Silvano is the white Arabian horse I bought last month. Pearce disapproved of my buying Silvano too. I found Silvano in a small town north of my ranch where he was trying to survive in a pasture of weeds. He was thin and his hooves were too long. A shoe was missing from a front hoof. I fell in love with Silvano because he was neglected and afraid and he needed to be cared for. I put myself in his horseshoes and I saw that he needed me. Isn't this the definition of love?

The ad I saw in the newspaper yesterday read: MUST SELL: 4-year-old Arabian gelding, gray, 15 hands, Egyptian blood, bred for endurance.

I called the owner of this horse right away. He gave me directions but I haven't been anywhere near this area. I have a strong feeling about this gray Arabian horse. I need to see him.

Pearce has never understood my love for animals. He feels a connection to me but not to my animals. He loves music and he has devoted his life to perfecting his skills as a guitar player. I fell in love with his creative spirit the moment I met him. He and I met through a group of musicians who put together a Flamenco band and then hired me to be the Egyptian dancer to feature their Arabic-Flamenco fusion. On stage surrounded by a dark sea of lively onlookers, Pearce and I would make love to each other through his music and my dancing. His fingers went wild on his high-pitched electric guitar, mixing Arabic music with rock and roll. My slender body responded to his frenzied melodies with swaying, vibrating and pelvic thrusts. We saw only each other as we performed. We sensed only each other as we moved with concentrated abandon. The audience was mesmerized by our sexual performance. We knew that in time we would find each other's bodies in the flesh and invent the same electric pulsation that we expressed on stage.

Pearce and I now live together at my ranch outside Santo, New Mexico. Historically, Santo was an artist colony that attracted painters, dancers, musicians and bohemians from all across the United States. It has been and still is a popular place for free thinkers to live unconventionally. Pearce and I both love Santo because the community supports and nourishes our originality. Our greatest joy is sharing our desire and appetite for each other's bodies. Pearce makes it a priority to buy wholesome food and cook wonderful meals. And we worship each other. We feast off our sex, merge into each other's souls and kiss with lips that crave each other's taste. We have a world of two. I am very much in love with Pearce and I know he loves me intensely. But he never accepts my need for horses.

Pearce is very practical. He wants to save money. I only want to live for the moment. I spend all the money I make on supporting my many animals on my ranch: dogs, cats, goats and horses. I keep reminding Pearce that I have always had lots of animals in my life, even as a child. I want him to understand that animals are my friends and have always been my best friends and companions. I'm not trying to hurt Pearce or frustrate his dreams because of a recent desire to have new horses to ride. I have always wanted a ranch full of animals. All day, Pearce has been trying to discourage me from seeing my new gray desire. Even now, he is trying to influence me to turn around and go home.

"But I need to at least look at this horse." Nothing will change my mind, not even Pearce's obvious hypercriticism. I can't help myself. It is my path to take. No one, not even the man I love and idolize can convince me that seeing this gray horse is a bad idea.

When I finally reach the address of the owner of this gray horse, there is no one home. I am defeated. I have to turn around and go home. Pearce suddenly begins to chat happily about our July 4th dinner together tonight. As a last attempt to spot the gray horse, I drive around the premises of the owner's house. All I find are a few skinny horses in a smelly marsh, none of which are gray.

"I wish I had the money to buy the horse that you want. But I just started my new day job and I need to focus on saving money. I love you, Toni. But I cannot support your animals. Please don't buy another horse. You already have three horses. You don't need another one."

"My old stallion and mare are together near the main house. Silvano is in a corral on the other side of the hill, out of sight of the horses. He needs companionship. Did you know that horses can die of broken hearts?" I cannot tell Pearce what I really feel. His new day job and his night job playing guitar in a jazz band keep him so busy that I see very little of him now. While Pearce is making money, I am getting lonely. When I complain that I never see him, Pearce gets irritated. As long as I don't complain that I never see him, he is happy with me. So, I need my own interests to occupy myself with while Pearce is working. I can think of nothing better than to have horses to ride.

My grandmother, Lula, bred and raised Arabian horses in Colorado. She gave my mother, Helena, a yearling Arabian stallion when I was eleven-years-old. I rode this young Arabian stallion, Khalifah, barefoot and bareback with a halter and a rope. This young stallion and I grew up together, riding past ponderosa pine and aspen trees in the mountains and galloping through expansive arroyos, dry river beds that became rivers during monsoon season in the summer.

When I was twelve-years-old, I found a little Palomino Shetland pony for sale. My mother gave me the fifty dollars I needed to purchase the pony. I rode the pony home. I called the pony Sage. I kept the pony in a corral near Khalifah. He jumped Sage's corral and mated with the pony. The result was Saida, a half Shetland and half Arabian horse. Saida has always been Khalifah's prized possession. Whenever I rode Khalifah, Saida followed in his hoof-steps. Once I was riding Khalifah with Saida right behind me and we rode past a mansion. The owner of the mansion was sitting on his porch in a big chair. He saw us riding by and he waved, smiled and shouted out to me 'You are so lucky!' I thought to myself as a young girl, 'Wow, here is a wealthy man living in his fancy house and he thinks I am lucky.' I never forgot this moment.

Now, Khalifah is retired. I stopped riding him when he turned twenty-seven-years-old. Saida is a pony. I need two horses so I can invite another person to ride with me. My deep hope is that, in time, Pearce will learn to love my horses and he will enjoy riding them with me. Riding horses in beautiful scenes of nature is my church of choice. It is a religious experience for me to be outdoors on horseback. To share this communion with the man I love would be my idea of heaven!

I wish I could depend on Pearce. My animals all these years have always been more expensive than I could afford as an Egyptian dancer. I have had a relationship with a drug addict named JJ since I was nineteen-years-old. He has always claimed that he is too dangerous for me to be involved with so our relationship has never been permanent or consistent. But he has always been generous with me. When he was prosperous, he always gave me money for my animals. He loves my animals, though he is never sober long enough to play with them. He doesn't mind that I buy things for my animals. In fact, he encourages it. He knows how important they are to me.

JJ always keeps his distance from me. He lives in New York City. He says he is addicted to big city action as well as to cocaine. JJ could never relate to my simple country lifestyle. He is like a big brother, supporting my love for animals and sending me extra money when he has it. In exchange, I try to encourage JJ to quit his drug addiction. I try to be an example of good health and fitness. JJ admits to me that he has very little beauty in his life. I am valuable to him as I am a source of natural feminine beauty to him. He is having a love affair with a drug: it is his mistress and his enemy, but he doesn't know it. I appreciate his support of my animals. Pearce knows that JJ helps me but I know it makes Pearce feel helpless and unhappy with himself. Pearce knows he cannot support me completely on his own. I need JJ's help.

Last Valentine's Day, Pearce gave me the emerald engagement ring that I always wanted. I lost it two weeks later. I was sick over losing it. Then Pearce bought me a second emerald engagement ring. I can't believe that I actually lost this ring also. I guess I am too active to wear rings on my fingers. I feel so terrible about losing two emerald rings. I know Pearce wants to marry me but I also know he will not accept my animals, especially if I buy any more. I wish I could depend on Pearce. I wish I could trust that Pearce loved me and valued me. But unless he values my animals, I know in my heart that he will never truly value me.

❦

"I just received photos in the mail of the gray horse I tried to find on July 4th. He is a beautiful horse. I want him! I want Silvano to have a companion. I will call the owner today and arrange to return to ride this gray beauty, if the horse is not sold by now."

Pearce says nothing with a frown. I won't invite Pearce to see the horse with me this time. I won't invite JJ either. JJ has recently come to Santo to visit me. JJ told me yesterday that he wants me to support myself in my own business now. He wants to quit working. He says he wants to find a whore and just travel around. I know he is high and I know JJ never remembers a word he says to me later. JJ loves to fight with me when he is loaded. I realize that I am easily dispensable to him.

I need to start depending on myself. I still get jobs dancing at Indian restaurants once a week. This is definitely not enough financial support for a ranch of animals. JJ once promised to give me a big truck to pull my horse trailer. Now he tells me he won't give me anything. He is playing games with my head. He is trying to make me feel weak so he feels almighty. He is truly a bully and a coward. Why do I even keep a connection with him? He is so high that he is cruel and he doesn't even know it. To compensate for the ill-will I have to endure from JJ, I crave my gray horse even more. I need more beauty in my life to outweigh JJ's loathsomeness. I want to buy this gray horse and ride him out of the degrading relationship that I have with JJ and his addiction to drugs. My vision is to buy a big truck to pull my horse trailer and load Silvano and my new gray horse and ride away from JJ into pure and natural environment where I am honored and safe. Is this too much to ask the Universe?

❦

My friend Thomas has just arrived to move some heavy dance mirrors for me. Thomas is a slender Italian artist with a head full of thick, black curls. He lives in Santo, making blown glass jewelry and sculpture. For the few years I have known him, he consistently tells me I am his muse. He is my biggest fan. I always see his smiling grin in the audience during my dance performances. He has never approved of my relationship with Pearce. He feels I deserve a man who treats me better than Pearce treats me.

"Guess who I just saw at the grocery store? Pearce. I overheard him talking to a friend who asked how you and Pearce were getting along. You know what Pearce said? He said 'I love my own space and all Toni cares about are her animals.' I thought you should know what he says about you behind your back."

"Really?" I guess I am not surprised. Pearce will always be unavailable to me: music is his first love and focus.

⁊

Here I am driving down the same dirt road but this time I know where I am going. I talked my mother into coming with me. Pearce refused to come with me a second time. I am actually relieved that Pearce is not sitting next to me as my mother loves an adventure. Today, there are groups of Latino men sitting outside their old adobe houses. They watch me drive my little truck slowly through their village. I am sure they don't often see two Anglo women driving by. I find the house of the owner of the gray horse and the owner walks out. I climb out of my little truck.

"Hi. My name is Sisco." Sisco is a Latino man with bushy black hair and a black handlebar mustache. He wears a white shirt, blue jeans and a brown leather belt with a huge silver buckle. His muddy cowboy boots give me the sense that he is a real cowboy. He is friendly. He shakes my hand strongly. I introduce Sisco to my mother. He invites us into his monster truck to take us to the gray horse. As Sisco drives my mother and I for a mile down a dusty dirt road, my heart beats rapidly with anticipation. I see the gray Arabian horse the minute Sisco's truck slows down by a big pasture.

"There he is, Mother!" I exclaim. I forget that I am supposed to act disinterested as this is the best way to buy anything in Latin countries if a person wants a fair price. But I cannot control my excitement. "Isn't he beautiful?"

"What a pretty gray horse," my mother says truthfully.

"Sisco, can I ride him?"

Sisco pulls out his saddle and bridle and he gets the young horse ready for me to mount. I notice that this horse bites but I decide that since he is only four-years-old, he'll grow out of it. The minute I get on the horse's back, I know that I want to own him. My heart is swelling with joy and pleasure. I am thrilled to the very center of my being. This gray horse has a spirit that is wild and unpredictable. I can feel that this horse will never be owned by anyone but himself. I want to have this unrefined energy in my daily life.

Since I can remember, I have dated men through the years who always break up with me with the indignant words, 'Toni, you are unmanageable!' I guess this horse mirrors my own untamed and impetuous personality. It is extremely bewitching to see my essence in a horse.

My mother once told me my first baby words were 'goatie' and 'pretty goatie' as my mother owned goats when I was a baby. Growing up as a young child, my friends were my dogs and cats, never other children. I rode my first horse by myself when I was nine-years-old. I was addicted to the smell and feel of horses from then on. My grandmother gave me a wild, chocolate brown Shetland pony named Leanova that I trained when I was ten-years-old. I rode this pony bareback up and down steep mountains, riding with a halter and a rope for reins. My mother also loves horses. She has three sisters that all rode Arabian horses with her when she was a young woman. My mother told me that when a man courted one of her sisters, the sisters would take this man on an exciting horseback ride in the wilderness as a test to see the true character of this man. If the man complained, found fault with everything or if he could not control the Arabian horse, this man would not pass the test and the sisters would not waste their time with him again.

My Arabian stallion was my best friend and companion all through high school. I never had friends in high school. I never even got asked out on a date. I used to ask my mother 'Why am I so ugly that no boy will ask me out?' My mother always told me confidently, 'You are not ugly, Toni. Someday, you will be beating off the boys with a broom.' I actually never felt really lonely as I had my horses to love me. I have consistently had better relationships with my horses than with any human being I have ever met.

This is still true today. I know Pearce tells me he loves me everyday but my old stallion is a combination of gentleness and strength that speaks to my heart more than any words Pearce could ever tell me. My old stallion is getting older every day. This young gray Arabian will help buffer the pain when my old stallion decides to pass on to horse heaven. I need this young horse!

I ride him around and he doesn't rear or buck. I feel certain that I can train him with love. Will he respond to my love and care? I am sure that he will. I know that I respond well to love and care expressed from other humans.

JJ's constant attempt to force me to do what he wants when he wants it only makes me hate him. He is a manipulator. When he is high, he gets violent. He tries to threaten and frighten me into doing what he wants. Fearing JJ only makes me want to be as far away from him as I can. He tells me he loves me, but his words of love only make me feel mistrust. He does not know how to make me feel loved and cared for. Neither does Pearce. Pearce gets angry and frustrated when I don't obey his guidelines.

My parents raised me to be a Bohemian girl. They believed in a philosophy of parenting called the 'turtle theory.' Turtles have their babies and then leave them. Baby turtles raise themselves. My mother went back to college when I was five years old. This is when I first remember preparing my own food. My mother always bought natural food. Whole wheat bread, honey, peanut butter, flat-bread crackers and butter and raw goat's milk were my favorites. There were never meals at a dinner table and so I could eat whenever I was hungry. There were never babysitters or anyone watching over me. There was no supervision and no curfew. I could come and go as I pleased. I could do exactly what I wanted when I wanted. I learned to care for myself, to fend for my needs and to find rides to places I wanted to go to. I started hitch-hiking when I was thirteen. I was a wild child.

I know most people don't understand wild things. To gentle a wild animal, a person needs to give constant, repetitive reassurance. The animal needs to feel safe from pain, attack and criticism. Trust needs to be earned over a long period of time. I know this for myself so I feel sure that I will be able to show this horse that I love him. He will someday be able to respond to my love with the same gallantry and loyalty that my old stallion shows me. When my mother agrees to buy this horse for me, I am delighted! With a flushed face and a racing heart, I arrange for Sisco to deliver this untrained horse to my ranch in three days.

∾

I am standing in my driveway, waiting for Sisco to bring my new gray Arabian horse to me. I have found a perfect name for this horse. Kamar. Kamar means 'the moon' in Arabic. Kamar is now four-years-old and gray with a black mane and tail. This is exactly how my old Arabian stallion looked when he was four-years-old. Through the years, my stallion turned pure white. Even his black mane and tail turned white as he aged. This reminds me of the cycles of the moon. The New Moon is black. The moon becomes brilliant white as the Full Moon. I want my new horse to learn to trust me and allow me to ride him effortlessly. I want him to be bright and enlightened like the Full Moon as he matures. I love his new name. It is appropriate for many reasons.

Oh, there he is! I see Kamar in the back of a flat-bed truck driven by Sisco. Kamar is so young and yet so regal. He has his head held high and his black mane and tail blow elegantly in the breeze. He is watchful with a daredevil look in his eyes. I can hardly wait to embrace his beautiful neck. Sisco unloads Kamar easily. I put Kamar in his new corral and watch as Silvano and Kamar meet each other for the first time, touching noses with heads to the sky.

My old stallion paces frantically around his corral, unhappy with the new male horse smell. Luckily, a hill separates my stallion and mare's corrals from the two gelding's corrals. Otherwise, Khalifah would feel constantly threatened having a new male horse to compete with. Khalifah adores Saida, his little mare. Even though I always keep them separated, the stallion and mare touch noses through their fence. My stallion's screams fill the air whenever she is out of his sight even for a second.

"Let's go to the Flea Market, Toni. I am looking for a good rope," Sisco says.

"My stallion is retired so he no longer needs his saddle and bridle. I use them when I ride Silvano now. But I need a second saddle and bridle for my new horse. Yes, I will follow you." I climb into my small truck and

I follow Sisco's big truck to the Flea Market. We walk the many isles full of booths selling jewelry and clothes. We spot an old cowboy from Texas with a booth full of old riding tack.

"Look at this old saddle." I find a very heavy saddle that is in good condition. The Texan cowboy tells me it is a saddle from the 1950s. I decide to buy it. I also buy a pair of buckskin chaps, a pair of white boots, a bridle, a halter, a lead rope and a breast collar. I am so excited. I can hardly wait to start riding Kamar.

"Sisco, please call me so we can go riding when you are in my neighborhood." Sisco agrees to call me sometime. I drive home from the Flea Market with all my treasures. I feel rich! I decide that I want to feed Silvano and Kamar a lot of feed so that they get strong. I need to get a big hay barn so that I can store large quantities of alfalfa and oats.

I call JJ when I get home to tell him about all the thrilling events of my day.

"I need to stay away from you." JJ is high. I never know what JJ is going to say to me when I call him.

"Fine. I will give you space," I respond as I always do. I hang up the phone in bewilderment. I guess JJ wants to be a disagreeable drug addict. He doesn't want me to help him to get sober. It makes him uncomfortable to have a straight friend like me. I have never taken drugs and I have never been drunk in my life. Even when JJ offers me drugs, I refuse with disgust. As a flower child of the 1960s, I have been exposed to many people high on pot. I saw a woman high on acid try to jump out of a top-floor window of a two-story house once. As a child, I watched people pass around joints. I was never offered drugs when I was a child. Even though I grew up around drugs, I always felt that drugs were a waste of time. Adults high on drugs seemed stupid and destructive to me. I never saw anything admirable or cool about the entire drug scene.

In high school, I was ostracized because I didn't drink alcohol or take drugs. I was the smart girl studying for her classes while my peers were out in the school parking lot getting high during lunch and going to drinking parties after school. I was never invited out to parties. For the entire four years of high school, I was never asked to go anywhere with anyone in my class. My classmates didn't like me because I didn't drink or take drugs. My senior class was grounded for drug use. Our annual senior trip was canceled. The boys in my class formed a group they called the 'bueno boys.'

They resisted authority. Being high or drunk was their trademark.

I found my identity with my stallion. Riding Khalifah after school every day was my greatest passion. To this day, I have never wanted to enter the drug world. I understand why JJ finds nothing in common with me. His entire life revolves around taking drugs. My entire life revolves around my animals. My animals are dependable and they don't abandon me on a whim. They are consistently affectionate and loving. They trust and respect me.

I have an older sister, Annie, who left home as a young woman to live in San Francisco. She got entangled with heroin addicts. My mother had to drive to San Francisco and search for Annie. My mother was desperate, trying to save her young daughter from destroying herself. My mother rescued Annie and brought her back home. But Annie still looked for homeless heroin addicts in Santo. She would bring them home and crash on the living room floor of our house with them. My sister, high on heroin, was violent toward me. She beat my arms and back with her fists and screamed obscenities. All through high school, I had to wear long-sleeved, turtle-neck shirts to hide all the purple and black bruises on my upper body. My sister also chased me outside, grabbed me, threw me down on the ground and stuffed sand down my throat until I was choking to death. My mother knew what my sister was doing to me. I begged my mother to intervene. My mother said, 'Your sister is the lamb and you are the lion, Toni. She is the weak one and you are the strong one. We have to help your sister.' So, I had to be strong. I didn't feel strong. My big sister continued to abuse me physically and verbally for years.

I grew up around drug addicts like my sister and drunks like my peers. Alcohol and drugs are familiar to me even if I abhor them. I have to remind myself to stop worrying about JJ. He is incapable of love. All he loves is his drug. I will focus on my new horse Kamar. I walk over the hill to Kamar's corral. Kamar walks over to me, eagerly. He is very sociable but he tries to bite my shoulders and arms. How can I train my horse not to bite? I realize that I have a lot to learn about this horse. I have never had a horse that bites. Kamar is aggressive and rambunctious. He wants my full attention. I stroke his neck and shoulders and I tell him that I love him. He is so beautiful. He is my visual vitamins. I sense that I need to convince him that he is safe with me and that I will never harm him. I need to gain his trust and earn his love.

꩜

"When you are loaded, you are repulsive and toxic to me," I tell JJ on the phone. He has just called me. I can tell that he is loaded.

"I want you to break up with Pearce."

"I won't! Pearce is trying to quit smoking. He is trying to quit drinking booze. He is willing to let me try to help him improve his life. He needs me!"

"Then I am not giving you a truck."

"Fine. I can use Brant's jeep to pull my horse trailer. Someday I will get a truck of my own. I want full control of my own life now. No one is my boss anymore. No one is going to tell me what to do and who I can and cannot be friends with. My life is my own path to take. At the end of my life, I die alone. I get to choose how to live my life!"

"I want a whore that I can run around with, then, if you won't be my girlfriend."

"You need rehab, JJ. Your whore is your drug. I can't depend on you. I need a boyfriend I can depend on. I need a boyfriend who helps me support myself. As a dancer and dance teacher, I barely make enough money to pay my utility bills. I have four horses to feed now. I need a secure income. I need a boyfriend who is nice to me. I refuse to talk to anyone, including you, unless you can be nice to me."

"I just want you to be honest."

"Your honesty is mean. I don't need cruel honesty in my life. I need a man who is sweet and loving to me. Go ahead! Find a whore that you can love. I need to go now. I have better things to do than fight with you on the phone. I have to fix the corral where my new Arabian horse pulled on it. And I want to start riding my new horse. I have good things to do with my life. You are destroying your life with your drugs and your addictions. You could never give me what I want. I want a sober man who is sweet, gentle and kind to me. I want a man who encourages me to be happy doing whatever I choose to do. I don't need a dominating, controlling and addictive bully like you. Don't call me again unless you can be nice to me!"

꩜

20

This is the day I plan to ride Kamar by myself for the first time. I walk to Kamar's corral and he moves towards me right away. He bites my arm and I push his head away. I pet his nose but he just wants to take a chunk out of my shoulder with his teeth. I need to teach him to stop biting me! He accepts the halter and I tie him to the fence. He doesn't mind my putting the blanket on his back. I get the saddle I bought at the Flea Market. It is very heavy but I lift it up on to Kamar's back. I have a snaffle bit bridle that he hates: he won't let me get the bridle over his left ear. I struggle with him until he finally submits to my persistence. He chomps loudly on the bit. Well, Kamar is saddled and bridled. I decide that to be safe, I should ride him around his corral.

I quickly get up on Kamar's back. What joy to be able to ride this wild young horse. How I adore his daring and impetuous energy. I ask Kamar to move forward. But Kamar chooses to buck. I manage to stay on but I am starting to feel afraid. We are standing by a pinon tree in his corral when he unexpectedly rears up. I am aware of the danger I am in just as I feel the tree branches on my back. Kamar has fallen over backwards into the tree. I am suspended by the branches of the tree as he falls to the ground. I climb out of the tree as I see that Kamar is knocked out on his side flat on the ground. He doesn't move. I touch him gently, shaking with panic. His eyes are open and he is breathing. He is shocked. I let him lie there on his side as I frantically unsaddle him. I realize that I have an inexperienced horse on my hands who likes to buck and rear up. He obviously lost his balance when he reared. His fall to the ground shocked him more than it scared me. The tree branches saved me from getting hurt. I give a prayer of thanksgiving to the tree. Then I help Kamar to his feet.

I think I finally see the truth: Kamar needs a lot of instruction. Do I know anything about training a horse? My old stallion never kicked, reared, bucked or bit me even one time. I am used to riding a perfect horse. How do I handle a horse who bites, rears, bucks and wildly throws around his head?

☙

"Can you rescue me? My jeep broke down thirty miles from your house. I need a new battery. Can you come and get me and drive me to an auto store? Then I'll need you to drive me back to my jeep. I can put the new battery in myself."

"I will be right there, Brant." As I drive my small truck to find Brant, I think about him. Brant is my favorite brother. Even though he is only a step-brother, he feels like my true family. I am an only child, conceived by a mother and father who married in Mexico and divorced two years later. My mother had already decided to leave my father when she discovered, to her dismay, that she was pregnant with me. For my mother, life with a man who didn't believe in running water and electricity in the house he built was too difficult. When she met my father, my mother had three young children under the age of eight from a previous marriage. My father had an illegitimate baby whose mother gave her newborn baby to my father before she left him to return to her husband. My father needed a wife for his infant son and my mother needed a husband for her three children. They both had similar ideas about living naturally and so it seemed like a perfect match in the beginning.

My mother discovered, after her marriage to my father, that he believed in intentional poverty. She hadn't bargained on this and it was too much for her to cope with. My father was also very amorous and my mother never got a moment's peace from his advances. He constantly wanted sex with her. I really sympathize with my mother's plight then. Here she is, a mother of three and now a mother to a new baby that isn't hers that she has to care for, living in a rugged one-room shack with no plumbing or electricity with a man that won't leave her alone. She is a strong woman for enduring two years like this. I admire my mother for living with my father for this long.

My father was an idealist. He had a mission to help third world countries with his inexpensive building material ideas and he wrote many books throughout his lifetime giving details on how a person can save money by building his or her own house. My father was a pioneer in the owner-builder arena. What finally killed him years later was the advance of technology. His philosophy of living close to nature was no longer revered by the country he loved. The greed, superficiality and materialism of the 1980s broke his will to live. He died as a physically healthy and robust man in his fifties. I believe it was suicide. Who will ever know if, during a violent rainstorm, my father intentionally went into a building that he built with a weak roof? The roof collapsed on him during the night. My older brother

Henry had to dig my dead father out of the mud the next day. It is a tragic story and one that I will never recover from. I know from this story that people like my father can lose their will to live in this world when their ideals are destroyed. I am grateful that my mother is healthy with a strong will to live. But I am not so sure about Brant's desire to live. I finally find Brant and his jeep on the highway. We talk as I drive him to the auto store.

"I had a fight with JJ. He refuses to give me the truck he promised me. I haven't heard from him since our fight and that was over a week ago."

"JJ must be on a bender, Toni. You know you never hear from him when he's on a bender. But don't worry. You don't need JJ to give you a truck. I have a strong jeep. We can use my jeep to pull your horse trailer."

Brant is the sweetest man I have ever met. He understands my love for horses. I met Brant when I was seventeen. Brant was twenty-two and had just come to New Mexico for the first time. He was eager to see my mother as he hadn't seen her since she divorced his father years ago, before she met and married my father. Brant was only my mother's step-son but my mother always bonded with the children she cared for even if they were not her own. Brant decided to move into my mother's little trailer behind our house. He used to help me with my Physics homework when I was attending high school. I had to maintain an 'A' average to keep my full scholarship there. I did hours of homework after school and studied every night. Brant was very kind to offer to help me with my homework as he knew that it overwhelmed me.

Luckily, I always managed to take some time away from the heavy load of studying every day after school to ride my stallion. I would especially love to gallop him on the mesa tops at sunset in the nearby Indian reservation. The moments riding my stallion were the moments I lived for. I felt perfect peace and complete fulfillment when I was in communion with my stallion and the elements of nature.

Brant and I lost touch with each other for many years after that initial bonding. A few years ago, Brant was given a high-paying job as engineer at a big company. The job was so stressful he suffered a mental breakdown. Now he is mentally disabled with bipolar neurological disease. He sleeps all day and cannot work. The only time he gets out of bed is to visit me even though he lives thirty minutes away. He hasn't shaved in years. He hasn't taken care of his body in years. He is an alcoholic. And he takes anti-depressant drugs to prevent suicide. He continues to attract women who take advantage of his inability to make decisions. These women try to run his life and take the little disability money he makes each month. I always wonder why my brothers are involved with overbearing women? Why am I always involved with men who criticize and condemn me and who undermine my dignity? I guess my brothers and I are sweet-natured people with big hearts. We would rather love the difficult people in our lives and give in to their needs and demands than fight them, defend our beliefs or leave them.

After I help Brant get his new battery, he follows me to my house. He agrees to go riding with me. I tell him I am very nervous as Kamar has already reared up and fallen over once. Brant reassures me that he will be with me if anything bad happens. I know that Silvano will relax Kamar out on the trail. Brant has ridden horses with his aunt in Montana: she raises Arabian horses. He has forgotten how to saddle and bridle a horse so I saddle and bridle the two horses myself. I decide to ride to a grove of aspen trees in the mountains three hours from my house. Kamar is perfect going up the trail. On the way home, he wants to buck and run away with me. Brant's company settles my nerves and I manage to keep Kamar from bucking me off. What a glorious August day in New Mexico! The sun shines persistently, glimmering through the tall trees around us. The cool breeze reminds me that fall is approaching. Brant and I talk and talk amidst the beauty of the mountain trail.

"I haven't heard from my brother Henry since last June. I thought Henry and I were close but I guess I am wrong. Henry never calls or writes me. I don't understand why Henry and my brother Ted both married bossy, dominating and controlling wives. How can they be attracted to this?"

"Men have needs to be mothered, Toni. Men often do not want to marry an exotic, exciting, desirable and attractive woman. This is too threatening for them. Most men are insecure and they know they cannot handle a woman that is attractive to other men. Men want to feel safe and so they marry the unattractive woman that will take care of them."

"This doesn't make any sense to me. A man has to look at his wife every single day. Wouldn't he prefer to look at a sexy and beautiful woman?"

"You are sexy, Toni. You are beautiful with a very exotic style. You are also very strong-willed and emotional. Men with no self-confidence feel you are either unobtainable or unmanageable. You are a challenge to men. Men prefer to settle for plain and unattractive women with unpleasant personalities. Or they settle for women that they can control. For example, most people usually buy horses that obey them. You bought Kamar who refuses to obey you most the time. Men would trade Kamar in for another horse. You are like Kamar. You are high-spirited and resolute. Most men cannot handle the fact that you think for yourself. You do not obey anyone unless it rings true to your own heart first. So once men realize your free spirit, they will always trade you in for another woman.

Men are also uncomfortable feeling passion and love for a beautiful woman. Men prefer to be in control of their feelings. Men's emotions get out of control around a resistant woman like you. So, men will reject you, in the end. They know they cannot handle their own emotions of jealousy, insecurity and lack of self-worth when they are around you. They know other men will always be trying to win your affections. Insecure men with low self-esteem cannot marry a beautiful, spirited woman with a mind of her own!"

"What about you, Brant? Why don't you ever get married?"

"I like living alone. I will never get married."

Somewhere deep inside my heart, I always wondered if Brant secretly loves me. Because he is my step-brother, he holds himself back. We are family. He knows it is taboo for a brother to love a sister.

"Brant, I want to find a real man to love me especially when I am unhappy and emotionally insecure. I don't want a man who only loves me if I am mothering him. I radiate health and so I attract men in pain. I attract drug addicts like JJ and alcoholics like Pearce. They want me to nurture them and I do. But I am actually very needy myself. I have compassion for deeply sensitive and wounded men because I am deeply sensitive and wounded myself. I need love and affection more than the average woman. I need a man who loves me enough to take responsibility for me. I always attract men who just want to use me and take my strength, my health and my sexual beauty so they get strong. They feed off my vitality like vultures. They give me nothing. And most men don't love my animals. I can't force a man like Pearce who claims to love me to love my animals too. But if a man doesn't love my animals, I feel he doesn't love me. My spirit is deeply bonded with the spirits of my animals. How can I find a man who I feel really loves me? Pearce tells me he loves me every hour of every day. Why don't I trust him?"

"You don't trust Pearce because you know he is very unhappy

within himself. His career as a musician is going nowhere. He is frustrated because he can't make money playing his guitar. He knows you are more accomplished, energetic and creative than he is. He disapproves of you and criticizes your desire for animals because he knows he cannot help you support them. He feels like a failure as a man and as a provider. He is living at your house, using your appliances and furniture. All he owns is his guitar. He knows you paid for your ranch with money you made as a Middle Eastern dancer. You are a success, Toni. He is a failure and he knows it. Every time he is with you, he is reminded what a failure he is. He feels worse and worse about himself every day he is with you.

He tries to control you to make himself feel more powerful. He tries to make you feel badly about the money you spend on your horses so he can feel self-righteous. He doesn't love you, Toni. If he truly loved you, he would encourage you and support you the best he could to do whatever it was in the world that made you happy. He will leave you in the end because you are too good for him. He cannot face his own failure in his life. You are nurturing him so he will get strong physically but he will never be able to support you or nurture you the way you need to be nurtured. He can only condemn you and try to bring you down so he feels better about his own life. He will leave you the minute you need him to nurture you. He is using your energy. He is a vampire, sucking out your inner joy."

"Oh, Brant! I love Pearce! I want to heal him. I hope Pearce appreciates my love for him and I hope he succeeds in his music career someday."

ↂ

"Pearce, could you ever accept my animals?"

"I love you. I love it when you take care of me. I love it when you cook for me. You are the only woman I will ever want. Your body is perfect for me. I don't even look at other women now. When women try to talk to me at my gigs, I ignore them. But if I wanted an animal, I would get an animal. I cannot take responsibility for your animals. Your animals are your domain. I didn't want you to buy Kamar. You went against my wishes. You are an independent spirit. You always do what you want, regardless of what I tell you to do. You must face taking care of your animals on your own."

I watch Pearce's face as he talks. He is frowning. His long black hair makes it difficult for me to concentrate on his frowning mouth. His long hair represents freedom to me. On a man, long hair is a symbol of divinity and strength for me. Pearce is such a beautiful man with such a breathtaking soul. I fell in love with Pearce's soul when I met him. People told me not to get involved with Pearce because he was a terrible alcoholic. He knew an older, wealthy blonde named Sheila who obviously had a crush on him. She followed him to most of his gigs. I could never compete with her wealth. One time, at a rehearsal with our band, I brought Pearce a protein bar as I knew he never had time to eat lunch. Before I had a chance to offer it to him, Sheila arrived with a large take-out lunch for Pearce. I was embarrassed to give Pearce my little gift until after the rehearsal. Pearce took it and said he liked it better than the fancy take-out lunch he had received. He made me feel that he appreciated the heart more than what money could buy. He knew I was not rich. Our connection was our love of music and dance. Our bond was that he knew I saw into his artistic soul. I saw the jewel beneath the unpolished exterior.

Now, I realize that Pearce doesn't have the heart that I need in a man. I feel that if a man really loves me the way Pearce claims to love me, his passion for me would make him accept my animals even if he doesn't love them. He would know how much these animals mean to me. I know that the man who really loves me may lack zeal for my animals, but he would have enough emotion for me that he would do whatever my dream needed. My dream is to have two beautiful Arabian horses to trailer to the mountains and to ride for hours in scenic wonder and natural harmony. My heart's desire is to be fused with horses and nature.

Pearce's passion is his music. His heart is truly unavailable to me as his heart is welded to his guitar. I give myself heart and soul to him but he cannot give himself wholeheartedly to me. As long as I am taking care of Pearce or obeying his wishes, he is excited about me. The minute I have my own needs or my own dreams, he rejects me with criticism. Pearce wants power over me. He wants me to be subservient to him. Even though he wants to marry me, I know his love for me needs to be tested.

One night when Pearce was drunk, he got angry with me and said, 'When you are my wife, you will have dinner on the table when I come home from work!' I will never forget this. How can I marry a man who just wants me as his slave?

I am not truly convinced that Pearce loves me. He just loves the woman that serves him, takes care of him and does what he wants. Basically, Pearce loves only himself. He has no interest in loving or caring for me and my needs. My animals are an extension of myself. If he cannot love my animals or even understand my need for them, how can I believe that he loves me? I cherish Pearce so I continue to hope that maybe some day Pearce will learn to open his heart and really love me for who I really am not just because he needs a woman, any woman, to submit to him.

I know that I have changed Pearce's life. Because of my positive influence on him, Pearce has given up alcohol and cigarettes. Pearce had been a chain smoker since he was fifteen-years-old. I named his lungs Blacky and Smoky and I talked to his lungs, telling them that I was so sorry that Pearce was destroying them. This technique worked. I think Pearce started to feel sorry for his lungs too. When I gave his lungs an identity, he started to feel guilty for the way he was ruining them. He understood that his body was a living entity. Pearce stopped taking his body for granted. He saw that there is more to life than playing his guitar with a cigarette in his mouth. His health became a priority and he wanted to take the time to care for his body.

I wrote up a body-building program for Pearce and taught it to him. I introduced him to yoga. I took him to a vegetarian health spa in Mexico for a month. I was the belly-dancer entertaining the international guests in the evenings. Pearce took long hikes and my yoga classes during the day. He decided to become a vegetarian as a result of this experience. I admire Pearce's ability to stop his self-destructive habits while he lives with me.

JJ has never respected me enough to consider quitting his drug addiction problem. Pearce is capable of change. Maybe someday Pearce might open his heart and learn to love my animals. Now, Pearce wants to buy a car. I know Pearce would rather save his money so he could buy a car than help me with my animal's feed bills. I can't seem to make enough money as a belly-dancer to support all my animals. Pearce's solution is for me to sell my animals. This is not an acceptable solution for me. I need my animals. They have all the love and affection that I have never been able to find in any human being. Not even Pearce can give me the tenderness and good feelings that I need and receive from my animals. He often gets irritated when I hold my little dogs. Is he jealous of them?

I may disagree with Pearce and he may disapprove of the way I spend my money but I stay with Pearce because I love his naked body. I yearn for

Pearce's soul. I am addicted to Pearce's manly desire for me. He lusts for me in a way that unites my soul to his soul through our sexual solidarity. Our love-making reaches me on a molecular level, down to the cells and tissues of my body. Pearce feels omnipotent when he craves my body. His virility and his desperate sexual hunger captivates my feminine mind. I watch his masculine member with awe. I worship Pearce as a Greek God when he is naked and demanding my body to please his physical voracity. I bring Pearce to sexual euphoria. I will perform any physical act to bring Pearce sexual fulfillment. Pearce always roars his rapture to the heavens at the moment of his release. I am thrilled to the very core of my being during the seconds of this cock cry. I want Pearce to desire my body more than I want him to love me. The words 'I love you' from a man have never meant much to me. I need tangible evidence so that the words have meaning. As much as I long for Pearce to want to provide for me and my animals someday, I fear in my heart that the most I will ever receive from Pearce is his need to be in control of me and my sexuality.

Pearce is irresistibly seductive in the bedroom but outside the bedroom, all we do is argue about money. I often feel Pearce's fear that he is getting too close to fire when he expresses his lust for my body. He may not be able to emotionally handle our electric intimacy. Is he afraid of loving me too much? Is he afraid of opening his heart to me too much? He can easily express his carnal lust for me but I always feel he keeps his heart hidden and unavailable. It may be safer for him to give his heart to his music than to give his heart to a woman. He wants me to marry him but I don't know if Pearce wants to marry me because he loves me and he wants to make me happy or because he wants ultimate power and dominion over me.

If JJ could lose seventy-five pounds, I could love JJ's body. But JJ has been so dependent on drugs for so long that the drugs have taken over JJ's soul. There is no sign of soul or spirit left in JJ's body. What I love in JJ is his beautiful, kind heart. I only see remnants of this heart when he is sober. He is so rarely sober that I often forget that there are any redeeming qualities in JJ at all. But JJ loves my heart and, unlike Pearce, JJ loves my animals. I don't think JJ approves of me getting Kamar though. JJ knows I cannot afford to feed Kamar.

JJ loves my dogs and my cat, Miss Kisses. Miss Kisses is a very affectionate, long-haired, black and white cat. Her first owner is a woman who loves cats but who is allergic to them. This woman had been getting allergy shots every week for two years. I guess the shots were getting more unbearable so the woman put an ad in the newspaper, looking for a good home for her cat. I answered the ad and now Miss Kisses is mine! Miss Kisses has a cat door from the back door of my house into the fenced-in back yard. She leaps through the cat door, stretches herself out under some sagebrush and watches the magpies and wrens as they squawk and chirp in the juniper trees. Then she hops back into the house and climbs the wooden ladder up into my loft where she tucks her paws under, closes her blue eyes and purrs in the sunshine. I am so grateful for her company!

⁊

"I am so glad you came to visit me! Look! Look how beautiful Kamar is!" I am riding Kamar around his corral. JJ is in a good mood. He is wearing baggy jeans and a huge dark green sweat shirt. His sneakers are dirty and the shoelaces are untied. His eyes are cloudy from drug usage but his smile is bright. His sandy brown hair glistens in the fall sunlight.

"I have decided to leave you a truck that you can use for the rest of August. You can use it to pull your horse trailer."

"Oh, thank you so much! Now I can take the horses to mountain trails in neighboring towns. This makes me so happy. I would like to do something for you in appreciation for your help. How can I inspire your life? I have tried for years to help you but you just keep getting more self-destructive. You gain more weight each year and you get deeper and deeper into your drug addiction."

"You can help me by taking care of yourself. I won't survive if anything happens to you, Toni. Even though I want to find another woman to spend my life with, I still love you."

"I know I am not your type of woman. You need a city girl and a woman who likes drugs, alcohol, excitement and travel. You could never settle down and be happy living with me on my ranch with my horses. It is too boring for you here. You like the city and action. You are addicted to adrenaline and a fast-paced lifestyle."

"You can live with your boyfriend on your ranch. I want to live in Australia. I need to be wild. I will always wish that I could change my lifestyle and lose weight because I always fantasize that you will be mine someday. But all I can do now is try to help you and treat you like my little sister."

"You know that restricting what you love destroys it. I need Pearce in my life. You cannot help me and then expect to control me. I accept Pearce's need for music just as I accept your need for drugs. You need to accept my need for Pearce even though Pearce refuses to support my animals. I appreciate your support of my animals. And I have fun with you. I will always remember the time I fell in love with you when I was nineteen-years-old and living in San Francisco. Remember? I was working at a health food store on Mission Street and you walked into the store and started talking to me about wheatgrass juice. You offered to give me a massage. I knew it was a come-on but I liked your cheerfulness and your big smile. I agreed to allow you to come to my apartment in the Haight. You gave me a deep massage that night and you were a perfect gentleman. You were so handsome and so sweet. It was easy to fall in love with you then!

But now you have destroyed your good looks with years of awful eating habits, lack of exercise and addiction to chemicals. I am not attracted to overweight men because it shows me how little these men care about their health. You have no respect for your body, JJ. I feel sorry for you. I wish I could help you but you refuse to be helped. Your life is so ugly now. I could never live in ugliness. I want beauty all around me and that's why I need Pearce, Kamar, all my animals and my ranch. Pearce has such beauty in his soul. He lets me teach him how to eat healthy food and how to quit his addictions to alcohol and cigarettes. He is open to letting me help him to transform. I wish you could let me help you to transform too. This is why I have never been able to marry you. I can't be married to a man who refuses to improve his health and who chooses such a sordid life. I cannot marry a junkie!"

❧

My hay barn is being built today. I am so excited! I will be able to order two hundred bales of alfalfa at a time! I will feel so rich when I have my hay barn full of alfalfa. I am going to hook up JJ's truck to my horse trailer. I have never driven a truck with a horse trailer before so I need to practice driving up and down my road.

Pearce is not happy about the money I am spending on my new hay barn. He admits that he feels inadequate because he cannot afford to pay for the hay barn. He gets irate with me because of his own feelings of insecurity. He condemns me for following my life's dream because he can't support me. Pearce spends more and more time at his gigs. I wish we had more time together. I know Pearce loves playing music more than anything else. He loves music more than he loves me. Pearce cannot help me do the things I love to do. His full concentration is on his music. The woman in Pearce's life will never be his priority. Sometimes Pearce is miserable with his gigs and then he tells me he needs me and I am the most important thing in his life. But this moment passes. Soon, Pearce is back practicing his guitar for hours, totally absorbed with his music. He expects me to be available when he needs me. When he is preoccupied, he expects me to entertain myself.

Part of the reason I need my horses, my truck, my horse trailer and my new hay barn is to have an equally absorbing passion as Pearce's music that occupies my time while he is busy. I always want a balanced relationship. I never want to love Pearce more than he loves me. I never want to need him more than he needs me. Having horses to maintain my happiness matches Pearce's obsession for his music.

❧

"Why can't we get Kamar into the horse trailer? We have been trying for two hours to get him in. We've tried to entice him into the trailer with apples and carrots. We've tried getting him in with a rope around his rear. We've tried everything we know how. He just won't go in! I give up! Let's just go riding around here." Brant agrees with my frustrated outburst. I can see by the sweat glistening on his forehead that he is just as worn out as I am from trying to get Kamar into my horse trailer. I need to buy some books on horse trailering. Or maybe I need to hire a cowboy to teach me how to do it. There has got to be a simple way to trailer a horse. I see horses in trailers being pulled by trucks on the highway every day. How do these people get their horses into their trailers? I thought horses just walked right into horse trailers. I never needed to trailer my stallion before so I admit I know nothing about trailer loading.

Brant and I ride for hours in the hills around my ranch. He handles Silvano perfectly. Kamar behaves badly on the trail when I try to ride Kamar by myself but when Brant is with me riding Silvano, Kamar is willing to keep up with Silvano. I think I need to buy some books on horse training techniques also. How can I train Kamar not to buck, rear, bite and run away with me? My stallion behaved perfectly his entire life every time I rode him. Kamar is a wild horse. I need to learn how to ride him. Do I need to hire a cowboy to teach Kamar how to behave?

⁂

Pearce is performing with his band at a bar in Santo tonight. He allows me to bring my friend Rita. Rita recently moved to Santo after her messy divorce in Louisiana. She loves living in her one-bedroom adobe casita. We met at a gallery opening where I was performing my Middle Eastern dancing. We became friends right away. She is petite with short brown hair and blue eyes. She is wearing a white shirt, blue jeans, red cowboy boots and a black vest that has fringe with crosses and beads that sway as she moves.

During a break, Pearce puts down his guitar and walks over to sit next to Rita and me at our table.

"Hi, honey. You sound good tonight."

"Hi, little sweetie. What did you do today?" Pearce kisses me sweetly.

"Brant and I tried to load Kamar into my horse trailer. We tried for a long time but we just couldn't figure out how to do it."

"I want you to sell the horse trailer," Pearce tells me bitterly.

"Do you like me?"

"Of course, I do. What an idiotic question. I love you!"

"You act like you don't approve of anything I do. Why?"

"Because you don't listen to me." Pearce stomps away. Rita is surprised at the way Pearce flies off the handle with me. Rita and I talk about her new life in Santo and listen to Pearce's band until the end of the evening. As the musicians are packing up their gear, I walk up to speak with the band's lead singer, Danny. Pearce immediately grabs me by the arm and forcefully drags me out of the bar with Rita following us in great distress.

"Toni, how many times have I told you to never talk to Danny about his personal life? Haven't I told you that Danny is a pathological liar and a womanizer? Danny lies to all his girlfriends. You shouldn't believe a word he tells you. I forbid you to ever talk to him again!"

I am humiliated and embarrassed that Pearce yells at me like this in front of Rita. I feel very cold and detached and I say good-bye to Pearce. Rita and I walk off together to my little truck.

"Pearce just hurt you deeply, didn't he?" Rita asks with concern.

"He disapproves of almost everything I say and do."

"He needs to control you, Toni."

"I won't be controlled. I am a free spirit! Having a wild horse like Kamar reminds me of my own wild spirit. I cannot be told what to do. Pearce is trying to force me to obey him and I won't do it! I am just like Kamar. This is a lesson for me, Rita. I need to learn how to work with Kamar somehow. I don't want to force him to obey me as I don't like the way it feels when Pearce is forcing me to obey him. I don't want to be a controlling person like Pearce. I don't ever want to be cruel to an animal that doesn't do what I want. I want to be gentle and loving. I refuse to hit or yell at animals even if they don't obey me. I would hate myself if I ever hit one of my beloved animals. Kamar often chases me with bared teeth. How do I stop him from attacking me? I need to be close to other horse lovers who understand horses. Other horse lovers won't condemn me constantly for owning and loving horses!"

෴

"Are you having fun? Isn't it wonderful to be riding the horses together, Pearce?"

"No. I am getting sun-burned and this saddle is making me sore. Let's go home."

"But you lift weights at the gym. How could you be sore from riding? We have only been riding for an hour."

"I don't like long rides. I don't want to go on a long ride on horseback again!"

34

"Okay, okay. We will go home now. But do you understand how much I love horses? I've loved horses since I was five-years-old when my mother put me on my first Arabian horse. All through junior high and high school, my best friend was Khalifah, my Arabian stallion. My love for horses is the essence of who I am. I am never going to change. I am not capable of getting rid of this love and passion for horses. Nor would I want to, even for a boyfriend. Do you understand this about me? Do you even care to know me?"

"You don't care for yourself very well. All your energies go towards caring for your animals. Can't you see how much money you spend on your horses? You should be spending this money on fixing your teeth. You know you need to get bridges and crowns on your teeth."

Pearce knows that I have inherited bad teeth from my mother. He knows I love sweets. It is impossible to argue with him because he knows how badly I need money to fix my teeth. He also knows how expensive dentists are. But how can I explain to him or to anyone that I don't even care about living this life unless I have horses to ride? Life would be intolerable for me without horses to ride into forests and mountains. I need to be in untouched, uncultivated territory and I need to be with powerful animal energy. Horses are primeval and archaic. I require the combination of being in unmolested, natural land on the back of a horse. Why is this so critical to my life?

I love Pearce's creativity. He loves music and peace. I want Pearce to flourish. But Pearce is too civilized, too cultivated for me to relate to. I would love to be with a man who shares my love of animals. Pearce honors technique, art, discipline and the rational mind. I desire unrestrained libido and raw emotion erupting from instinct.

JJ loves animals and he enters into undisciplined territory when he takes his drugs. But he has no guidance. His drugs are poisoning him. He descends into darkness, breaks down and never breaks through into enlightenment. His drugs are killing him. He admits he is doing excessive drugs. He admits he is a junkie. And yet I need him. Ironically, JJ appreciates me the most. JJ wants to lose weight and get into shape. His heart is still hopeful. He hasn't given up. I am his inspiration. I am the only beauty he has in his very unattractive life. His drugs have consumed him. He is incapable of natural pleasure. The constant chemical stimulation of his drugs force JJ to require even more excitement for him to feel anything at all. Natural beauty, grace and charm are absent in JJ's life. But he sees me and he recognizes my genuine beauty and my love of nature. He craves this in his own artificial life. He helps me support my craving for horses and in exchange, I support his craving for my untainted femininity. So yes, I need JJ even though I respect and admire Pearce's ability to transform.

JJ tells me he'd be dead without my loving heart. This is true. There can be no love in JJ's heart as I know he is disgusted with his body, his unhealthy eating habits and his nasty drug addiction. Beauty and love cannot exist where there is disgust for oneself.

My love for my horses brings me daily joy. When I am happy, I love myself and my world. My heart is overflowing with love for my horses. I find extreme pleasure in my daily life. I renew my internal enchantment with life everyday when I care for my horses. It is my pure love and happiness that is saving JJ's life. Without it, he would have no connection to real emotion. He would die of an intentional overdose as his life would be too unbearably empty for him.

⁊⁊

Oh my God! I am falling off Kamar into a tree again. Kamar rears so high that he falls over backwards. He plunges to the ground and he doesn't move. I fall into the tree. I am scraped by the branches but as I climb out of the tree, I see that I am not hurt. Kamar looks dead. I have a carrot in my pocket so I put the carrot in front of his nose. He moves his lips to grab at the carrot. Kamar is not dead. He is stunned.

I manage to undo the saddle while he lays on his side on the ground. Once the saddle is off and he has gained his composure, Kamar struggles up to his feet. Now I am thoroughly afraid to get back on Kamar. I resaddle him and walk him home. I decide I must hire a cowboy to train Kamar. I don't know how to ride a horse that I am afraid of. Once I get home, I unsaddle Kamar, brush him and put him into his corral. I walk into my little house, determined to get help. I call a cowboy friend named Douglas.

"Hey, Douglas. This is Toni. My young horse just reared and fell over backwards again. I am not hurt but I am really afraid to ride him now. I need a cowboy to help me train Kamar."

"Do you feed Kamar sweet feed?"

"Yes."

"Well, the molasses in sweet feed makes a horse 'hot.' Stop feeding him sweet feed and he'll calm down a lot. How often do you feed Kamar?"

"Once a day."

"Start feeding him twice a day, once in the morning and once at night. Horses get bored and they need to be busy eating, especially at night."

"Would this prevent Kamar from chewing on wood the way he does?"

"It certainly will help. Kamar needs more activity. Can you get a long rope and lunge Kamar in a circle?"

"Yes, I can do this. Thank you so much, Douglas. You have given me great advice."

"And Toni, if you get desperate, I know a young man who works at Encantada, the dude ranch near your house. His name is Mike and I hear he trains horses. You may have to board Kamar at the dude ranch for a month while Mike trains Kamar."

"What a great idea! I think I will call Encantada and talk to Mike."

❧

"Mike, thank you for coming to my house. This is my horse, Kamar."

Mike is young, thin and soft-spoken. He wears a black t-shirt, tight blue jeans, old black cowboy boots and a big brown cowboy hat. He takes Kamar's lead rope and Kamar bites Mike on his arm.

"No!" Mike asserts himself. He pulls out a nail from his jean pocket and holds it between his fingers so the sharp point is up. When Kamar tries to bite Mike again, Kamar pricks his nose with the nail. Kamar pulls his head away with surprise. I see a tiny stream of blood erupting from Kamar's nose. I watch Mike handle Kamar. He rubs Kamar's neck slowly and gives comforting praise when Kamar is attentive.

"Toni, Kamar is a good horse with bad training. He bites out of a need for attention. I need to teach you never to kick him, pull him or force him to do anything. Never use a crop. Get Kamar to move by clicking your tongue. Say 'Walk' when you want him to move. Say 'Whoa' when you want him to stop."

I have never seen such a gentle yet forceful man in my life. What a combination! Mike shows me that there can be both kindness and strength in a man.

ↄ

"Why are you so mad, Pearce?"

"I overheard you flirting with Mike, your horse trainer."

"But Mike makes me laugh. We flirt openly, not in secret. I'll never go out with him. Flirting is harmless. It makes me feel good. I like being admired and flattered. It's playful and trivial. I'm sorry I can't please everyone in my life, including you. You push me away from you even more if you are irritated with me. You are not going to change me." Let Pearce be upset with me. I have to be myself and have fun in my life even if Pearce disapproves.

"I am going to spend the night in the studio next door. Oh, and by the way, I've been meaning to tell you that I plan to travel soon. I am going to save all my money for the next record I want to make."

Now I realize that Pearce intends to leave me for his music career. And he doesn't intend to spend his money on our food or electric bills. He wants to save his money for himself and his future record. When Pearce tells me that he is going to spend the night alone in the studio, I realize that he is unhappy with his life and with me. He is annoyed that I spend my money and time on my horses and not on him. On our first date, Pearce told me that he is used to women supporting him and he warned me that he'd never support me. I understood this and I reassured him that I could take care of myself. But I realize now that I need a man's support.

I don't admire a man who has no desire to provide for his woman. I don't like the way Pearce collects wealthy women as his groupies so he can get things from them, like free memberships to the gym where he works out and fancy dinners. His wealthy fan, Sheila, owns expensive dressage horses. He prefers to ride her high-priced horses in a ring than go riding on my lively Arabians in the mountains. This hurts me. I am not his wealthy fan. I am his artistic and spiritual equal. Even if Pearce disapproves of me, I have to be myself. I disapproved of Pearce's alcoholism and chain-smoking when we first met and he changed his health and his body so I would like him. He no longer gets drunk and he quit smoking and now he lifts weights everyday in a gym. But I cannot change the essence of Pearce. He will always like the attention of wealthy women. Pearce has to be himself also.

℘

I am in my bathroom on a Sunday morning. I am putting on my mascara, looking intently at my face in the mirror. Pearce walks in without knocking on my bathroom door. I see his face in the mirror behind me. His brown eyes look like daggers and his mouth is rigid and sullen.

"Toni, you never want to spend time with me anymore. I have to work more than ever now because you don't work enough."

"Any money that you make, you save for yourself, Pearce. Don't blame me because you work too many gigs. Your music is number one on your priority list. Do you think loving me non-verbally through long-distance is love? I don't. I need tangible love consistently."

"It's your problem, Toni. You cannot retain love. I give you love but you don't believe me and you need love all the time. Your heart is a leaky bowl. You are the one with the weakness."

"If you want to stop giving me love, I don't want to be with you anymore. You act like we are just room-mates now. You want your own life. You want to sleep alone in the studio. You want to make money for your own record."

"I thought we'd perform together and get jobs together. But all you want to do is ride your damn horse, Kamar!"

"Don't you ever curse my beautiful Kamar! You are so grumpy these days, Pearce."

"Shut up, Toni! Shut the fuck up!"

"Don't you ever talk to me like this!"

Pearce lunges at me and pushes me up against the bathroom sink. He grabs my neck with his long fingers and he begins to squeeze my neck with an iron grip. I am shocked! Pearce is strangling me! I have never seen him so cold-blooded. I quickly jab his knee with my knee and he releases his hold on my neck. He scowls at me, red-faced and ugly. I see the repressed rage coming out in his dark eyes as he glares at me with fury. Pearce is striking out at me because he has no outlet for his aggression. He is striking out for the sake of striking. He is unhappy with his life and his earning power. He is jealous of my little ranch. He feels inadequate as a man when he is with me.

He is in conflict. He is familiar with rich female groupies supporting him and yet a part of him is longing to mature and learn how to support a woman he loves. His repression of wrath has replaced his previous alcoholism. Now he is a dry drunk. His resentment and anxiety have driven away pleasure, tenderness and laughter between us. Pearce is violent with me and wants combat. He needs an opportunity to fight with real adversaries. He needs combat with other men, not with me. I am his lover! How dare he try to strangle me, the woman he loves! I suddenly see that Pearce can strangle me because he carries suppressed animosity and because he doesn't really know what true love is.

"Pearce, I have made up my mind that you should find your own place to live. I don't want to live with anyone ever again. Living with a boyfriend destroys the romance in the relationship. I want romance, desire and passion in my life, not violence and hostility!"

"I am not moving out! This is my house now too!"

"This is my home, my land and my property. You will move out when I tell you."

"The only way you will get me to move is to give me back the money I've invested in the mortgage for the studio."

"What? You have been paying rent, Pearce, not mortgage payments! I took out the mortgage with my credit to build the studio. It's my studio. I owe you nothing. You would be happier without having to pay rent to me. You would be happier without trying to support a woman."

"If I leave your ranch, Toni, I will never want to see you again."

"Our relationship has always been a sacrifice for your ambition. I cannot sacrifice my happiness for your happiness. Our relationship now is not what I want. I'd rather have our relationship the way it was when we first met. We loved each other so much when we first met, Pearce. What happened to this love? I never should have let you move in with me. I'll never make this mistake again. I am afraid of you now. I am afraid of your rage and disapproval. I want to follow my life's path in peace now, without your constant negative judgment of me. I want to go camping with my horses. I want to ride Kamar all the time!"

"I will move out in three months if you still feel this is best. I would want to move out if I got very disappointed in you. Stop nagging me about spending time together."

"Fine. I will give you three months. And I won't beg you to be with me anymore. I'll let you be as cold and as distant as you want. But you need to keep paying me rent if you live here. And you won't ever see this rent money again. I can't tolerate your resentment towards me. I can't put up with your intellectualism. Even your religion is lifeless and unfeeling. At least you know I want you to leave. Now you can start looking for another place."

"I try to give you my advice, Toni. You think it is criticism but I am trying to help you. You aren't familiar with male advice because you never had a father. When I give you suggestions, you feel threatened. You rebel. I am trying to be fatherly and loving when I am giving my advice."

Pearce has a point here. I have never experienced having a father. I was never blessed with the love of a father. My mother left my father before I was born. I met my father for a few hours for the first time when I was five-years-old. And I didn't spend any time with him until I was eight-years-old. I visited him, his new wife and my younger brother and sister in California for a month in the summer. I was the visitor. My father never touched me and rarely talked to me. I used to watch my father laughing and playing with my little sister on the couch in the living room while I stood in the shadows behind the door. I was hoping to have a relationship with my father when I was older but my father died.

When my father died, I couldn't understand how I could still be alive when my father was dead. My father created me. I yearned for masculine energy and attention all my life because of this huge deficiency of fatherly love. I still crave masculinity to fill this void in my heart. Will my heart ever be whole and full? Or will I desire stable masculine love endlessly every day of my life? I never feel satiated or satisfied with a boyfriend's love.

For my entire life, I have been around men who are incapable of loving me. As a result, I am not fond of the human race. I have tried to love by giving everything of myself, hoping to get love in return. I don't. Men grab and pull for my love. I no longer want to be subservient to abusers or trapped in a bad relationship. If I have to ask for love or demand love, it's not worth it. I am tired of the power struggle between men and women. Does there have to be continual war between demanding men and giving women?

I see now that I feel my own emptiness and I am seeking fulfillment through my partnership with Pearce. I try to lose my sense of impotence in devotion to Pearce's body. His body gives me sexual pleasure and the possibility of blissful merging. My awareness of my inner space makes me feel empty, hollow and hungry. I crave to be filled. I am susceptible to dependency on an outer impregnation. I am losing my loneliness in the bliss of melting into my love for Pearce. I need to be parented by the masculine because I have never had a father. I crave Pearce as my lover yet I yearn for a father figure in my life. The shadow of Pearce is the part of him that strangled me in the bathroom. This shadow is bull-like passion, raw desire, power and demonic bullying. Pearce is trying to overwhelm my femininity with his stubborn defensiveness. He is struggling to control and hold his own without caring where he destroys our playful sensitivity and empathetic relatedness.

My addiction to Pearce's love is not satisfying to me. What I really need is union with my masculine father. My heart is wounded yet I try to heal men like Pearce and JJ who both have serious alcohol and drug addiction problems. I try to heal myself with the crumbs of love and appreciation that Pearce and JJ give me. I am not truly uniting with any man. My pain is for my father. I yearn for connection with my father. When I am with Pearce or JJ, I am getting back at my father and also getting pieces of my father back. Pieces are not enough for me. Pearce is not bringing into our relationship enough of what I've lost with my father. Pearce cannot provide for me. He doesn't acknowledge me for who I am. My illusion is that I'm going to get Daddy's love. I never learned to love myself because my father never loved me.

Pearce has no perception of my inner pain. I want to feel capable of expressing this torment to him. I want to tell him that he is not giving me what I need to feel truly loved and cared for. All my anguish is totally cloaked when I am with Pearce. Only my teeth are my true identity. 'Dental' and 'identity' share a similar meaning to me. My teeth need to be repaired so that I can bite and chew and express my needs for sustenance. I need real substance and real food that I can digest and feel sustained with. Pearce does not give me the food I need. I love Pearce but his love doesn't nourish me. He will always struggle to be a musician. He cannot care for anything but himself.

I want so much to be confident within myself. I need to find the love that feeds my heart and makes me feel cared for and happy. The main thing that gives me substance in my life is my unbroken horse, Kamar, even though he frightens me with his out-of-control behavior. Every time I try to ride him, he unnerves me and I have to get off and walk. He challenges me like nothing else. I am determined to learn how to earn Kamar's respect and love for me. Riding Kamar with assurance will be the first step towards finding my inner strength. I have decided to board Kamar at Encantada so Mike can work with him.

✧

"Sit back in the saddle with your legs forward. Good. Now stop pulling on Kamar's reins so tightly. Keep loose reins. Allow Kamar freedom to move his head. When you want to stop him, pull back on the reins gently for a second only and then release the reins right away. If he wants to trot, let him. Let him enjoy you being on his back. Let him express himself and not feel tied down and restricted all the time. You need to relearn how to ride a horse!"

"You are right, Mike. I have to learn how to ride all over again with Kamar. Should we keep using the bosol or should we use the snaffle bit?"

"Let's use the snaffle bit. Kamar should be old enough to use a bit now."

"Why does Kamar run away with me when he hears sudden noises? Why does Kamar freeze up when he sees things he's never seen before? He scares me constantly. I never know what he's going to do from moment to moment."

"Kamar has very little confidence. He feels your lack of trust in him so he is afraid, nervous and unsure. Toni, you are the one who needs to build up your self-confidence so Kamar's fears don't affect you. Your certainty will give Kamar assurance."

"I want you to look at my horse trailer, Mike. Can you teach Silvano to get inside? I can get Kamar into my horse trailer a lot easier than Silvano."

"It will take me a day of training but I can teach Silvano to get inside the horse trailer. He just needs to feel more comfortable when he is inside the trailer than outside the trailer. I will make Silvano run around in a circle and only let him rest when he puts his head in the trailer.

I hold Silvano's lead rope in my left hand and I lift this hand with my head looking inside the trailer. Then I walk in place to encourage Silvano to walk in. If he doesn't respond, I'll swing the end of the lead rope with my right hand in circles. Or I'll tap the horse's back with the end of a long stick. This will teach the horse to walk in the trailer. If he doesn't go in, I'll make him run in circles outside the trailer again until he is ready to stop and try to go in. I will start training today. Looking at your trailer, you need to hire a welder to weld more pipes to separate the two compartments. You need to weld pipes to prevent the horses from being able to turn their heads around once they are inside the trailer."

"Does my trailer need a platform for the horses to walk on up into the trailer?"

"I think platforms are dangerous. Your trailer is better off without one."

"Can I watch you train Silvano today?"

"Absolutely! I need to teach you how to safely load Silvano yourself. It is a big responsibility to own a horse especially if you want to trailer load horses and transport them on highways without mishaps."

"When can we take Kamar to Encantada? I need you to work with him more. I know you don't think he needs to be broken. But Kamar needs to be disciplined because I am too afraid to ride him now."

"Yes, Kamar needs to be disciplined. Let's take Kamar over later today after I teach Silvano to get into the horse trailer."

❧

"JJ, I love Creamy Snowflake! She is beautiful!" JJ has just arrived, bringing me a gift. My gift is a tiny, white, long-haired teacup Chihuahua. It is amazing to see how Creamy adores JJ. She wants to sit on his lap. When he takes off his ragged denim jacket, she immediately walks over and curls up inside it. This shows me that JJ truly does have a good heart even though he has been on a bender. I feel a mixture of many conflicting emotions because of his surprise visit.

"Toni, I want to see you suffer so I can watch and see what people around you do to help you. I could buy you a business. My cousin just died and left me a lot of money. I could give you millions of dollars. But I want you to make me your primary boyfriend. I will let you have lovers but I want you to make me first."

"JJ, you have to give up the drugs. They are destroying your body."

"I will go into rehab someday."

"No, you need rehab now. I want health and beauty in my life. You are ugly and ill."

"Then I am going to back off from you."

"I need you, JJ, but you are a big-time drug addict now."

"You have no time for me. You don't want me. I am going to bail out."

"Your self-pity disgusts me. You are loaded on drugs. You don't even remember what you say. You insult me, lie to me and try to make me mad. It's a waste of energy to talk to a drug addict like you. You can rant and rave all you want. You are a junkie. You know this. You will always try to bring me down. And you won't give me any money so I am always desperate and insecure."

"Why should I give you my support when you are with another man? You've told me how Pearce feels the rent money he gives you each month is an investment into your land that he wants back when he leaves you. This is crazy! Pearce is just using you for a place to live. He's a sponge and a loser. All he cares about is himself. Yes, I want you to suffer until you decide to marry me. Then I will give you everything I have. I am frustrated that you have a boyfriend."

"Pearce loves me. He just bought me a sapphire ring because he's committed to me. Pearce is the reason I love sex now. Pearce gives me the emotional comfort and support that you can't. You just yell at me and tell me that you like to see me suffer. Pearce is handsome. You have destroyed your body with your drugs. I need emotional support as much as I need financial support. I respect and admire Pearce and this is more than love. By giving me Creamy Snowflake, I see your worthy heart. But I can't help but see your repulsive body and nasty habits as well."

"I can't quit the shit now. In fact, I'm taking pills too. But I have millions of dollars and I won't give you anything because I don't want Pearce to get it. I want you all to myself before I give you anything."

"JJ, you just told me you wouldn't mind if I had a lover. You've been telling me to find a boyfriend for years as you claimed your lifestyle is too dangerous for you to have a girlfriend or a wife. Well, Pearce is my lover.

Pearce is beautiful and I won't give him up. Your girlfriend is your drugs. You are always on the shit. How can I be your wife? I won't be any man's wife unless this man is sober and healthy."

"Then I am going to find me a whore."

I start to cry. I cry quietly and then I gradually begin to sob with great shudders. I am hyperventilating. JJ will do what he wants. There is no telling him what I want. I am crying out of stress, fear and frustration. JJ would rather keep his drug habit and leave me than go into rehab. I have to accept his lack of commitment to me. JJ just wants to torture me and make me feel great distress because he is feeling self-destructive. He wants to destroy my happiness because he lives a wretched life of drug addiction. JJ's life is chaos.

I pray that Pearce's love for me will be stable, consistent and sweet in the future. I hope I never lose him. I need him. I need his beautiful body. I pray that I can make my own money someday. I want to find a website designer and create a website for my dancing. If I make lots of money, I won't need to depend on JJ. I want to stay with Pearce forever. I want to be true to Pearce. I also want to be a powerful woman on my own!

∾

"I want to take you on a road trip for the afternoon, Toni."

"JJ, you are high on drugs. I can't stand it! You are high all the time now."

"I promise I will not do any more drugs on this trip. Please. I need to talk to you." I agree to go with JJ even though I am apprehensive. I pack a few things and get into his fancy red sports car. He drives north. He is quiet. He drives to a small town, goes to a hotel and gets a room. I have known JJ my entire adult life. He is like my brother. I trust him and I follow him into hotel room #266.

Suddenly, JJ is enraged. He turns to me and bellows, "I no longer want to be with you!" I am terrified. He is threatening my safety and I begin to cry. Now I feel that JJ no longer cares about me. Without warning, JJ grabs at me, holds my body down and yanks off all my clothes.

"No! No, JJ! No!" I scream with desperation. JJ drags my struggling body toward him and unzips his pants. His pants fall off and I see his member swollen and hungry. He thrusts himself inside of me and I shriek with pain. Again and again, he thrusts, violating my womanhood with his sexual assault. He rapes me endlessly. He uses my thin body to masturbate his overweight mass of flesh. I weep, helplessly. He is too high on drugs to release so he finally pulls himself out of me so he can do a line of cocaine. He has never done lines in front of me. Now I see that he has no respect for me whatsoever.

"You are right, JJ. It is time to call it quits. I want you to take me home now and I never want to see you again. You just raped your best friend and sister. I will never forgive you for this. Take me home immediately!"

"Listen to me. I put a tag on Pearce. He is screwing a lawyer that is a man. Did you know your handsome lover is a fag? And Pearce is giving weight training lessons to a rich old lady at his gym. He is screwing her too. He is conning rich women out of their money by screwing them. Danny, the singer in Pearce's band, got paid lots of money to tell some Hells Angels about Pearce and his lawyer lover. These Hells Angels went to Pearce's gig and asked Pearce about you. He said he doesn't have to use condoms with you. So, Pearce thinks he can fuck you without condoms. And he's intentionally exposing you to sexually transmitted diseases and you think he loves you? If Pearce tries to take your land away from you or take money from you, I am going to cut off his hands! Do you hear me? Does Pearce know that my family is mafia? My people want to kill you and your family, Toni. You are taking advantage of me and refusing to marry me. The only reason you and your family have been spared is because my mother and father like you. Your older brother has been approached and warned not to hurt you already. Do you know his wife has a few lovers? Do you have any other lovers, Toni?"

"Stop this! Stop harassing me! You are insane. This is too crazy. Of course, I don't have any other lovers besides Pearce."

"You are a liar. I'm going to kill you."

"No! Please, JJ. Don't do this. You're high. You don't know what you are doing. You are not yourself."

"If I don't kill you then your mother will be killed if you ever talk about me or my family."

"I promise you. I will never talk about you to anyone!"

"Your mother will be killed if you ever talk to Pearce about me."

"I understand, JJ. Please let me go. Let me go home!"

"Don't you see? I want to marry you, Toni. I will pay you a million dollars if you have my baby. I want to get you pregnant."

"I cannot marry a man I am terrified of. I don't want children. You have terrorized me, hurt me and abused me more than any man I have ever known. You just raped me."

"You are just a retarded cry baby." JJ throws me on the floor as I sob hysterically. He rapes me again. And again. The third time he rapes me, he releases with a grunt. He pulls away from my body and zips up his pants without emotion. My body is a mess on the floor, raw with pain. My face is a blob of snot and tears. I try to get up off the floor but I can't move. I lay there, hopeless and inert. I know JJ has taken me prisoner because he is high on Quaaludes. These downers mixed with cocaine have caused him to lose his mind. His irrational malice makes me feel panic and deepening alarm.

"Will you let me live, JJ? Will you promise not to kill me?" I plead.

"I can't promise anything. I want you to marry me."

"I cannot marry a man who rapes me. I cannot marry a man who threatens my life."

"Then I don't want you to marry Pearce. He will take away your land. He is a con."

"I won't marry Pearce. Just promise me you won't cut off his hands."

"I won't hurt Pearce if you get him to leave you. He is a deadbeat. He is not good enough for you. Get rid of him and I won't hurt him."

"I will let Pearce go. But promise me again that once he leaves me, you won't harass him anymore."

"I promise I won't bother Pearce as long as he leaves you." JJ drives me home. I am worried sick about what he might do to hurt Pearce or my mother. He could kill them. He is a threat to my own life and he could kill people that I love. I decide that I need to tell Pearce. I need to protect him. I will tell him what happened to me today. He will know what to do. He will protect me from JJ. When JJ lets me out of his car, I run into my house, traumatized and relieved to be alive. I will never go anywhere with JJ again! I will never trust a word he tells me again. He is a rapist. I need to protect Pearce and my mother from JJ's mafia family. I am an emotional wreck now. I collapse into my bed, too exhausted to cry anymore. I sleep to escape my misery and grief.

I now see how JJ is living in lies and delusion. Everything he says is a lie. JJ wants me to tell Pearce his fabricated lies so Pearce will leave me. I have decided not to say a word to Pearce about anything that I just went through. JJ wants to marry me so he can own and possess me like his sports car. He will do anything, even rape me and scare me to death to try to stake his claim on me. He is forcing me to frighten Pearce away from me. But it won't work if I don't believe JJ's lies. Pearce couldn't be a homosexual. Pearce loves me. JJ is lying about tormenting Pearce. He is lying about his family being involved with the mafia.

JJ is a coward. He won't hurt Pearce. JJ is a bully. Bullies are deeply insecure. JJ would give up on me if I married Pearce but I can't marry Pearce. He is a dry drunk.

This is a nightmare.

The phone is ringing. I answer it reluctantly.

"'This is JJ. I am going to send you a check in the mail so you can start your website. And I am going to buy you the big truck you need for your horse trailer."

"This is just compensation for the emotional and sexual abuse you just put me through."

"No. You win. I am very mean to you and I need to apologize. But if you got pregnant, would you have my baby?"

"What? I don't believe in abortion so I would have to have your baby if I got pregnant. But I know I won't get pregnant. I will not spend time with you again unless you go into rehab. I am afraid of you now. You have threatened to kill me and my family. You are torturing me and verbally and sexually abusing me. You have told me for years that you wanted to protect me from crooks and criminals and now you are the biggest brute in my life. I need someone to protect me from you now. You blackmail me to do things I don't want to do, you manipulate me with things you give me and you threaten to take them away if I don't submit to you. You endanger my life and the lives of my loved ones. I will never trust you again. I will never marry a monster like you. But I will help you get into rehab."

Pearce has come home. His long black hair is loose, hanging around his smiling face as he greets me lovingly. I pray I haven't gotten STD's from JJ. I know JJ is not sexually active with women because he is extremely unattractive. His lover is his drug. I pray I am healthy as I revere Pearce's body. Pearce takes me into his body-builder's arms as he kisses me passionately.

"Please be careful when you are playing music in Santo," I whisper.

"Why?"

"Just watch out for the Hells Angels, okay?"

"Okay, sugar. Do you know I desire you more than any other woman? In fact, there are no other women in the world for me but you."

"What about all your past girlfriends and your two ex-wives?"

"What girlfriends? What wives? You are the only woman I have ever known," he jokes.

He takes me to my bed and lovingly removes my clothes. He gently makes love to me. I long for Pearce's manhood to be within the interior of my femininity. I love Pearce's body to be wrapped around me. Pearce teases me and tells me I am his playing field of sex. I laugh softly. How different it is to be with Pearce who makes me laugh instead of with JJ who makes me sob in terror. Pearce desires my body. He idolizes my long dancer's legs, my flat stomach, my firm breasts and my muscular back. He cups my round buttocks with his hands as he enters me from behind. His erection is solid yet he is attentive to my heavy breathing. He thrusts inside of me with a continuous pattern of many rhythmic shallow strokes followed by one deep stroke. He releases and howls wildly. I love his abandoned cry. With this primal masculine cry, I know without a doubt that my womanly body satisfies every cell of his yearning man's body. He holds me and kisses my parting lips with tenderness I have never known before.

"I love you, Toni."

"I love you too." How can I hide the horror of what I have just experienced with JJ from the man I share my body and soul with? If I tell Pearce what JJ did to me, will Pearce leave me? Or does he love me enough to stand by me?

"Pearce, have any Hells Angels approached you lately?"

"No."

"Have you ever slept with another man?"

Pearce chuckles. "I have never even had gay or lesbian friends."

"Do you work out with Sheila at your gym?"

"I rarely see Sheila at the gym."

"I am frightened. I need your strength. If someone attacks you, please fight back. Please protect yourself. I don't want anyone to hurt you, Pearce."

"Don't worry, sugar. I can take care of myself."

&

I am learning that men don't love me without also detesting my power of sexuality over them. They adore me and they hate me at the same time. I see that all the men in my life are crippled emotionally. The men in my life don't really know me. JJ thinks he loves me but he's drugged out. I project my erotic sexual energy on to men who I believe will help me. But neither JJ nor Pearce can really help me. I don't deserve to get abuse from men. Men are murdering my deep beauty. They are hacking me to pieces. I give my love too easily. JJ will never give me any power. He can only see his own needs. It's a delusion that any man will give me anything. I have to do it for myself.

I give away my inner resources to men when these resources could create ways for me to make money for me to live on. No man should own me. I won't tie my future to any man. I don't really need any man to back me. Men just use me. JJ gives me gifts but I owe him nothing in return. He can never buy me. There is nothing I can do to help him. Nothing he could have paid me would be worth what he did to me in room #266. JJ is using my weakness for his advantage. I need to stop giving my vital energy to crippled men. It doesn't bring me joy or pleasure. JJ is dangerous the way he is now. I need to help JJ get into rehab. He needs help. I pray he doesn't turn on me again.

I walk next door to the studio where I know Pearce is practicing his guitar. He always practices for at least four hours a day. I don't like to interrupt him when he's practicing. I open the studio door. Pearce is meditating, sitting cross-legged on his blue cushion on the floor.

"Pearce, I have something I need to tell you."

"What is it, little sweetie?"

"JJ raped me."

Pearce's eyes rapidly turn black with shock. Will he be understanding? Will he give me the emotional support I desperately need? Will he back me? Will he help me?

"You are deceitful. I feel abused now too."

"Please. I need you to understand that JJ threatened to kill me. I need your love and support." I reach out to hold him but he pushes me roughly away.

"Don't touch me! You disgust me. How dare you touch me? How dare you let me make love to you without telling me that your body is defiled? You might have STD's now. How dare you put me at risk without telling me? How dare you keep accepting gifts from JJ when he is a rapist? I don't want to touch you ever again!"

"I need your love. Please don't be so cold to me. If you can't handle me and if you can't touch me, you will have to move out. I know that JJ is selfish and cruel. He needs to go into rehab. He is trying to bully me into marrying him. He has only mentioned marriage to me in the last few weeks. Before this, he said he'd never marry me. He encouraged me to have a lover and to be happy with a man who loved me. But his drugs are making him irrational and violent. He's threatened to kill me and my mother. He's threatened to kill you or cut off your hands. He's just trying to scare you away. You aren't going to let JJ succeed in scaring you away, are you?"

"I need time alone. I am furious with you."

"If you cannot love me, then you need to move out."

⁊

"Mike, how is Kamar's training going? Sisco, Kamar's previous owner called me and gave me the vet's name that gelded Kamar. I called this vet and he sent me the receipt and the date of the castration. Kamar is definitely a gelding."

"I think Kamar must be naturally aggressive then. I've been making Kamar do what I want, like pick up his foot or back up before I pet him. And I have been using split reins instead of using neck reining. I need you to learn how to ride Kamar with split reins. Kamar responds better when you control him with a separate rein in each hand than if you use one hand holding both reins."

"I can't ride with split reins."

"Well, you are going to have to learn. Kamar is better about not biting or rearing but he still likes to buck when I take him out on the trail. He's a young horse. I think you should use this Tom Thumb bit for his bridle. And you need to use spurs and a crop. You might want to order a Vice breaker. It is a collar made for aggressive horses. It has an electric zapper that you push that shocks the horse when he is doing something bad like biting or kicking. I am not going to charge you for the last month of training because I don't think the training I did is going to stick. I am not going to work with Kamar anymore because I think you should sell him. I know someone who will help you sell him, Toni."

"I will take him home now. I am sorry you feel like Kamar is a hopeless case. I will try to ride him every day now and see if he gets better with daily riding. I don't want to sell him. I love him too much. But thank you for working with Kamar."

"Keep in touch." Mike walks away and I realize there is not much more he can do for Kamar or for me.

છ

Pearce is driving me to Santo to see my dentist. I just took the prescribed Valium for the appointment. The dentist has to put a gold crown on an upper tooth today. This appointment will take all afternoon.

"I've been thinking, Toni. I will stay with you if you promise me that you will never see JJ again."

"I have already told JJ that I never want to see him again. JJ told me he'd die without me. He promised me that he'd go into rehab if I helped him. I told him I'd help him. I am afraid of him when he is high, Pearce. When he is high on drugs, JJ is dangerous."

"If you don't stop seeing JJ, I am going to leave. And I want the mortgage money back when I leave."

"The money you gave me is rent money. I won't pay you back!"

"I deserve my fair share when I leave!"

"It's not right to ask for money from a woman, Pearce! JJ has given me money to help me support my animals through the years. He has never asked for his money back. And you want me to pay you money? It makes me feel you don't value our time together. I want you to stop giving me rent."

"If I stop, how will you pay your monthly mortgage?"

"I will have to rent the studio to someone else. I love you, Pearce. I love your beauty. All the men in my life are unattractive compared to you. But I need a man who wants to support his woman."

"I will only stay with you if you see your therapist and start being honest with me. The only reason you are tied to JJ is because of the huge expense of your horses. If you sold your horses, I could support us just fine."

"Pearce, I know you can't and won't support my animals. And I won't sell my horses. I need my horses. I know that my life without you will be empty and lonely. JJ disgusts me. I know that I am in financial trouble. But selling my horses is not an option for me. I helped you when you left your wife, when you needed a place to stay and when you were in trouble. Why can't you help me now? Can't you remember all the good things I did for you when you were the town drunk? Can't you remember all the years of love we've shared? JJ cannot destroy our memories."

"Well, I am not going to have sex with you until you get an AIDS test. And I want all your STD tests taken."

"I will get my tests taken this week. But the results will take two weeks to come in. I have to go to the County Health Clinic."

"We will be platonic friends until the day your tests come back negative."

"I will miss your affection."

"That's your problem."

"You'll be glad. Your sex drive goes lower and lower the more hours you meditate each day. You know that I need your love, Pearce. You are just going to punish me. This is not love! Love is bringing confidence and security to a loved one. Love is gentleness and sweet loving words. Love is trying to see life through your lover's eyes. Love is not making another person learn what you want. Love is earning someone's trust so this person feels safe learning something new. Love is wanting to make another person happy. Love is doing whatever it takes to keep harmony, peace and sensitivity alive. Love is not abuse. Love feels good, safe and warm. Love is caring and showing comfort and support. Love is not neglect, indifference and coldness. Love is reaching out, not pulling in. Love is extending your hand not retreating into your cave. Love is reassuring. Love is giving someone hope and joy. Love is building up a person's confidence with gentle strokes of calm security.

Now I wish I had never told you the truth about how JJ raped me. You demand honesty but when I give it to you, you freeze me out with severe chastisement. I told you because I was worried about JJ hurting you. I should have kept my mouth shut. You can never be kind and understanding, can you?"

"I have been trying to build our relationship. I hate playing music with Danny now. But I loved our nation of two so I play with Danny for the money. For you and me. I have learned that women like money. I need to have money to have a woman. But now I feel I have nothing."

"I can adjust to spending less and having less. I just want to keep my animals. I want you, Pearce. I want your love. I want our success together."

"I honestly don't believe a word you say. I am no longer attracted to you. I don't love you anymore because you deceived me. You betrayed me. I want you to give me JJ's full name and address."

"Pearce, it is best if we end our relationship. I cannot give you JJ's address. I will leave you alone now. You can stay as a renter in my house until you find a new place to live. I will try to stop loving you. I will try to give you your space and get my love from my animals. Our love is over. I guess I told you about JJ because I really did want you to move out. JJ ruined our relationship because it was already shaky. You were already critical of my horses and you were unwilling to support them in my life. I have been sick of your lack of tolerance for a long time. You are an ego maniac. I am tired of always massaging your body and stroking your ego. I need a man who massages me and adores me. You can be an austere and unforgiving dictator away from me. I will let you find your own place. The only benefit of having you live with me now is that it prevents JJ from taking over my life."

"I have lost the woman I loved. I have lost the life I loved. But you are living in shadow and I won't live in darkness with you. I'm going to leave you."

"You only see me as evil. Don't you remember my qualities and my light? It was this light that inspired you to quit smoking and drinking alcohol, start meditating and practicing yoga and working out, becoming a vegetarian and taking care of your body. Are you going to speak badly of me to others?"

"I won't."

"Well, if you think I am so sinful, you will move out willingly. I still love you, Pearce, but I don't trust your love for me. And you will always want to be a poor musician, unable to care for anyone or anything. I cannot live like this. I love your heart and your soul. But your mind is frigid and intolerant. Your body is freezing up. I will no longer wait around for you to give me crumbs of your attention. You view me as evil. Your heart is full of hate now."

"I am going to have dinner with Sheila tonight."

"What a hypocrite! Here you are telling me that I am deceitful and then you are going on a date! You are lying to me about Sheila. I know you are lovers with her. Your brother told me years ago that you and Sheila are lovers. Since you no longer love me, you have one month to live here."

"Fuck you, Toni." Pearce throws me the finger and drops me off at the dentist's office. He pulls his car away from the office with a squeal. I watch Pearce drive away with fuming speed. I am so foggy in my brain now from the effects of the Valium. My mind has separated from my body so much that I can hardly stand up to walk inside to see my dentist.

చ

JJ has just called me on the phone. He calls me over ten times a day now.

"Do you want me to go to a rehab near you, Toni?"

"JJ, you have to want to go to a rehab for yourself, not for me. All you ever tell me is that you don't want to quit your drug addiction. But you are violent when you are loaded."

"I've been high our entire relationship...twenty years!"

"When you are high on cocaine, you act differently than when you are high on crystal meth or downers. Whiskey affects an alcoholic differently than wine."

"Stop talking about drugs on the phone!"

"I don't care what you do, JJ. Do what you want. Just stay away from me."

"You have known for years that I want to marry you."

"No, that isn't true, JJ. You have never wanted to marry me all these years as you insisted that it was too dangerous for me to be associated with you."

"You led me on!"

"I never led you on! You said I was like your little sister. You said I was your family and this is why you helped me."

"I gave you money so you would want to marry me."

"I gave you my friendship and my love the best I could all these years. But don't you know how revolting you've been to me lately? Your unhealthy lifestyle has destroyed your good looks and your body. You have destroyed the man I fell in love with when I was a teen-ager. I had to really concentrate on your good heart to endure being near you. I sacrificed my esthetics to be near you."

"I don't see it this way. I am not going to buy you a truck to pull your horse trailer until you are smart enough to use it. And I want to give you a cell phone."

"I don't want a cell phone."

"I'm not going to give you a truck unless you have a cell phone."

"Stop arguing. Stop trying to make me rough. I'll never be rough."

"You need to learn how to be smart. You are retarded."

"I just want to be loved."

"You can't tell who is worthy of loving you."

"This is true."

"You are stupid and you protect your abusers."

"You are so full of hate! Your heart may be overflowing with hate but it doesn't mean I have to feel this way myself. I want love in my heart. I hope you don't hurt me again. You are ugly and evil. You are a demon. You ruined my relationship with Pearce. You raped me. You were my best friend most my life and then you raped me. I am barely able to eat now. I am anorexic and full of despair and sadness because of you."

"I will buy a house in Santo. I will try to help you now that Pearce is leaving you."

"I cannot handle seeing you when you are high."

"Well, get rid of Pearce and I will give you everything I have."

"I don't want your drugs in my life."

"I want to get you medical insurance and help you support your animals."

"I need peace and quiet to heal my body. I can't handle being scared, threatened or pushed around. You are too rough for me, JJ. I need you to put yourself into a rehab center. This is the only way I can deal with you. I will get strong with a healing environment, with the presence of my animals and with horseback riding in nature. Your drugs are not good for me. When you are high, you destroy me too. You break everything you touch. I need time to heal."

☙

Pearce and I are having dinner at my house. I have prepared shepherd's pie, Pearce's favorite meal. He loves it when I cook dinner for him. The pie smells delicious, hot out of the oven. We sit down to eat together in my small kitchen. This hot pie is my peace offering.

"I will not tolerate JJ in your life. I am watching you to see what you do. I will stay with you if you tell him to leave you alone." Pearce stares at me with strained determination.

"I cannot tell JJ what to do, Pearce. I am trying to help him. I am deathly afraid of him now. Maybe he will leave me alone now that I have become so thin. I know all my ribs are showing."

"Your problem is that you have no values. You don't know anything about honesty."

"I just have different values than you. I have to be true to my own self. I have to protect my life and try to help JJ get into rehab. You are trying to manipulate me as much as JJ. You both make me feel miserable."

"I am conservative. I have high values. I am strong. I am nothing like JJ! You need to put a restraining order against him."

"A restraining order against JJ will only make him lose his temper. He will kill me. Even my mother agrees that I need to help him and convince him to go to Israel or Australia and let me heal in peace on my ranch. You may have high values but your self-righteousness is downright merciless. Your excessive pride is reprehensible."

"It's over between us, Toni. I hate everything you represent."

"Here I thought there was hope for us. Now I see that you have no commitment toward working things out with me. I am not your girlfriend anymore. You don't want me. You don't want our connection anymore." I begin to cry quietly. I realize with sudden clarity that there is no hope trying to soften Pearce's heart.

"You can do what you want now."

"Fine. I let you go. You resent my horses anyway. You resent my happiness with my horses. You resent my love for my animals. You just want to hurt me and treat me like your enemy."

"God help my enemies." Pearce stands up to leave.

"You are cruel! I won't live with a man who treats me like I am ugly and unattractive. You can move out now!"

"I am looking for a place. I just want you to know I'm not going to have sex with you for another six months after you have an AIDS test and this test better come out negative! I better not get any diseases because of you!" Pearce is standing with his fists clenched as I sit at the kitchen table in front of him, crying.

"Don't worry. I will leave you alone. I won't try to get love from you. You can do what you want. I am on my own, remember? We have nothing in common anymore. We rarely even eat meals together. I need to get rid of you and JJ! You both make me unhappy. I will never live with another man again. I will concentrate on building up my life. I will focus on my horses, my dancing career and my website. No man will control me again. I will get strong. I will have my peace and quiet. Since you no longer believe in me, you are poison to my self-esteem. I will find people who appreciate me. I will spend lots of time with my animals."

"You bother me. I will never trust you again."

"You can't give me what I need. You don't have what I need to be happy. You blame me but it's really your problem. You have no money. You are arrogant and sexless now. I need more than what you have to give me."

"No, I can't afford to take care of you. People think I am taking advantage of you, Toni. But I can give you nothing. I refuse to touch your body again. You are a murderer!"

"What?" Has Pearce lost his mind? Who have I murdered?

"I will only stop calling you a murderer if your AIDS test comes back negative!"

"I was raped, Pearce! How does this make me a murderer? Why do you want to call me nasty names? Because you feel so hurt? Could you ever love me again?" Why do I still try to appeal to Pearce's heart? I know I have lost him forever.

"No, I will never love you again."

"You may be an attractive guitar player on the outside but your dark soul is sick with poverty and oppressed cruelty. When I ask you to help me with my horses, you refuse. You don't like to get your precious fingers dirty.

I need a man who isn't afraid of using his hands. You are always telling me how to live my life. Then you humiliate me if I don't do what you want. Be careful. You give lectures to people about their lives. You think you are the authority on values and morals now that I got you to quit drinking and smoking. People won't like you if you put down their lives and demean their ways of thinking."

"I believe in honesty. I believe in the conscious mind."

"I believe in protecting people I love. I believe in the heart. I hurt you but JJ forced me to. You are a tyrant and a perfectionist. Your extreme honesty is repulsive because you are so blatantly severe. Can't you soften up? Can't you feel sympathy?"

"I want to be harsh."

"Don't you know that the meek shall inherit the earth? I want to live my own life with my animals, separate from the human egos of the world. If you want to be holier-than-thou and condescending, I need to get away from you. I want to be with a man who is quiet and sensitive, the way you used to be. I can't keep loving you when you won't touch me. Once you move out, I'll be glad to be single so I can find a man who is gentle, humble, helpful and uncomplaining. You make me miserable. You have no feelings for me at all. I can't live with a man who isn't attracted to me. I fell in love with your body and spirit. But I despise your mind. If I had a million dollars when I met you, none of this would have ever happened. I needed JJ for financial help. You can give me nothing, especially now that you no longer love me. You are a musician. You will always put your passion into your guitar first and foremost, above all things. I want a man who puts his passion into me! I accept the fact that you are no longer my soul-mate. But I still want to love you in my heart even if you are hateful to me."

❧

I call JJ. I need to see a doctor. I am worried about my sudden weight loss. The Santo County Health Clinic where I got my STD tests done wants me to see a rape counselor who specializes in trauma.

"JJ, will you put me on your medical insurance?"

"I won't do anything for you unless you make me your primary man. I want you to marry me."

"I will marry no man. No man will ever own me. Do you think I could marry a bully like you anyway? You are a demon ego. You have bossed me around long enough. I will never marry you. My only safety with you is if you go into rehab."

"Don't forget I gave you Creamy."

"I love the part of you that gave me little Creamy Snowflake."

"Toni, don't you know that I'm a fighter? My family sells weapons."

"You are living in a delusion."

"If Pearce doesn't leave you, I am going to hurt him."

"I hate what comes out of your mouth."

"You should be raped a few more times, Toni. You need to get smart."

"You are cruel and inhuman and I will never forgive you for saying this to me. You like to make me cry. You like to make me miserable. You like to see me suffer. You are destroying yourself and I won't let you hurt me anymore. I hate you!"

"You can spit on my grave."

"You turn love into hate, JJ. You are crazy, drugged-up and out-of-control. I won't see you until you go into rehab."

"I want to visit you. I want to see Creamy."

"You have turned all my love for you into hate."

"I just want to share what I have with you."

"I won't take anything you give me unless it's in my name. You give me gifts and then you take them away when you are violent. I won't be your friend unless you go into rehab. Do you know that I called your mother? I told her that you are a dangerous drug addict and that you have been promising me for years that you want to go straight but you never do. You have never gotten healthy or lost weight like you promised me. Now you are taking Quaaludes which are making you insane. I told your mother that you raped me, JJ. I told her that I reported how you raped me to the Santo County Health Clinic when I got my STDs done. I haven't pressed charges hoping that you would go into rehab. I told her how I have no desire to spend time with you. And your mother understood. She said she couldn't control you either. I suggested that your cousins intervene and force you into rehab. You are a danger to yourself and others. She let me talk to your father. Your father told me he heard I wasn't well. I said I had health problems and I needed help. I told him I needed an environment of healing. I told him you are violent and you threaten my life and my family's lives. Your father sympathized with me and said he would try to keep you away from me. I told your father I would stand by you if you went willingly into rehab. This is my bottom line."

"I will go to outpatient rehab."

"This is not good enough."

"You have to learn how to share what I give you."

"You are just trying to change the subject. You manipulate what you give me to control me. No thank you! I'd rather have my freedom. You act like a thug." I realize that as much as I try to influence JJ into going into rehab, he just won't do it. Not on his own. Can his family force him to go?

∾

Pearce left to Chicago for a week. I feel so much more relaxed now that he is gone. I love Pearce but I realize that I cannot live my life to please him anymore. I decide to ride Kamar. It is snowing and windy. I pull on my pink long underwear, warm jeans and a thick black sweater. I thrust my feet into winter boots. I grab a warm scarf and a hat that covers my ears. I have missed riding Kamar. I haven't been feeling very strong or energetic lately. I have lost so much weight I feel weak. I need to exercise Kamar. Without my attention, he is only getting wild.

Once I am outside, I find a new burst of enthusiasm for my life. Even though I have two men in my life now who are uncompromising oppressors to me, I have peace away from them when I am with my horses. Kamar is waiting for me by the fence. He allows me to put the bridle on his head even though the bit is cold in his warm mouth. I should remember to keep his bridle in the house to keep the bit warm for days like this. He doesn't mind when I slide his black blanket on and lift his brown leather saddle to his back. I elevate myself up into the saddle with the stirrup and I am on Kamar's back. I decide to walk him around his corral a few times. The wind is causing Kamar to spook at the swishing trees. Kamar is nervous and lively as the snow falls everywhere around him. Should I take him out of his corral? I decide against this idea. I just ride him around and around. I practice using split reins. I turn him in circles. I back him up.

In the corral, Kamar accepts my directions. How I love to ride Kamar! How I long to ride him out on the trail. Will this ever happen? I don't dare to do this now. I am afraid of Kamar's inconsistency. This horse is jumpy around cars, dogs, blowing branches, noise and even big rocks. I need to find a way to teach him how to be brave in the outside world. I need to find a way to be confident when I am riding this horse.

I get off Kamar. I unsaddle and unbridle him. I stroke his beautiful face until he tries to bite me. I let Silvano and Kamar run free together in the corral. I watch in awe as they gallop madly together, chasing each other, rearing and kicking with abandon and joy! What magnificent spirit and beauty they have! How I long for joy in my own life. How I long to feel free to do whatever my body and my instincts tell me! I realize that my horses are my teachers. They keep me aware of a level of happiness that does indeed exist even if I have never felt it in any relationship with a man for any length of time. My horses are keeping me alert to a delight in living that I can aspire to. I pray silently: "Divine Powers! Please help me to find pleasure and liberation in my life someday soon! Help me to be successful with my dancing and my website so that I can support my little ranch! Thank you from the bottom of my soul!"

I am so tired of serving men. I am exhausted from holding up the mirror so that men can see into their souls. I know that Pearce needs his freedom to pursue his music. I know how unhappy he is as a musician in Santo. Santo is a small town and he hates the band he performs with. He is so much more fulfilled when he plays music in Chicago where he is now. I truly want him to find satisfaction with his career. The misery he feels with his unsuccessful career as a guitar player is destroying our love. His inner demons play with his mind and he blames the existence of his demons on me. But these demons are his whether he will ever admit this or not. I am just holding the mirror so he can see his interior clearly. I am unjustly being blamed for his own deep-seated feelings of inadequacy. I don't deserve to be any man's scapegoat. This is what prevents me from wanting to eat. I cannot eat when anyone in my life tries to make me feel like there is something wrong with me or the way I think, feel or act. Maybe I need to live by myself now. Maybe I need to get both JJ and Pearce out of my life so there is an opening for a new man to enter my life who can honor my spirit, relate to my soul, connect to my heart, encourage my thoughts and reassure me that I am important to him. This new man must never stifle my love for nature and animals, especially my passion for horses. As

I watch my playful horses, I know that my greatest wish is for my animals to thrive and for me to get strong again. If I am powerful, no man could control me.

༉

The phone has been ringing every ten minutes all morning. It is now noon and I am so annoyed that I finally answer the phone.

"It's JJ. I have an idea. Why don't you become a stripper so you can support your animals?"

"I hate you for even suggesting this." I hang up on him. What does JJ think of me? That I am a piece of raw meat for vultures to destroy?

JJ calls again. I don't answer. He leaves a message: "If you don't pick up the phone, I will call Pearce at work. I know where he works."

I answer the phone when it rings again.

"Toni, I have been trying to get you to marry me for years."

"You are such a liar, JJ. If you really wanted to marry me, you would have tried to lose weight, get healthy and get straight. You treat your male buddies better than you have ever treated me. You give them tens of thousands of dollars. You pay their bills and buy them houses. You have always claimed to be addicted to action. You have always encouraged me to find another boyfriend. You are a cruel and hateful junkie and you are not welcome on my land or in my life. You pretend to care for me but you are manipulating me with your gifts. I won't take any more gifts from you. I want my freedom. I will buy my own truck for my trailer someday. Leave me alone! I won't see you or talk to you again unless you go into rehab. I need to focus on my positive thoughts and dreams!"

JJ hangs up on me and I decide to write him a letter. Talking to JJ is a waste of my time. He is stubborn and incapable of reflection. Talking to JJ leads nowhere. His uncontrolled violence is without limits. His excess knows no boundaries.

"Dear Devil: I can't afford to pay my phone bill so I won't be calling you again. Any correspondence is now through the mail. The man I once loved in you is now possessed by the devil. If you want to contact me again, you must go into rehab and exorcise the devil out of your body and heart. You are incapable of love. You once tried to help me the best you could.

For the last month since you decided you want to marry me, you have hurt me, abused me and bullied me until I cannot tolerate one more second of your ugliness. You were nicer to me when you let me be free to be happy. You cannot force anyone to marry you. If you want someone to marry you, you need to try to be attractive, loving, kind and worthy of having beauty in your life. Now you tell me I should be raped a few more times and that I should strip for a living. Any man who says these things to me is the devil. Anyone would agree with me. I don't know how I will survive without the JJ who loved me. But I will have nothing to do with the devil who possesses him now. The devil that is you is not welcome at my home or at any place I go. If you try to force me to see you, I will scream for help. My family does not welcome you on their land. Stay away. You are pure repellent now. You are the devil and you belong in Hell. Going into rehab is your only chance of finding any spiritual virtue and learning how to be a loving human being again."

I mail this letter in Santo. I decide to look into getting a restraining order against JJ. I go to a woman's medical clinic and get a copy of a restraining order. A woman helps me fill it out. I take it down to the city judge, Judge Jordan. I have to wait all afternoon to see him. I am finally ushered into his office. I hand him my restraining order and he reads it over quickly. He peers at me over his spectacles and says "You have written criminal charges against this man called JJ. Do you know that if I sign this, JJ will be served a copy of this and he will be forced to come to court in Santo? You will have to face him in court."

"I see your point, Judge. Here I am trying to keep JJ away from Santo and these papers only force him to come to Santo. I guess I won't have you sign them after all. Thank you for your insight."

"You can keep this unsigned restraining order and bring it back any time you decide you want me to sign it."

"Thank you, Judge."

I drive home, grateful that I met an honest judge. I am amazed at the stupidity of the law. How can women protect themselves against men like JJ?

⁘

"Toni, I have found a place to live. I may move out right away," Pearce says indignantly.

"It's better if you leave."

I get into my little truck and drive to Santo. I have made an appointment with my therapist. My tears blur my vision as I drive. I know this is not safe.

"Sit down, Toni. Here are some tissues." Mrs. Yender is pretty with short blonde hair and big brown eyes that express her feelings openly. She is wearing a pale blue dress and white high heels. She looks concerned for my welfare.

"I am so grateful I made it here," I exclaim, sniffling as I wipe my tears away with the white tissues.

"What just happened to you?" she asks quietly.

"Oh, Mrs. Yender! My life is a shambles. I am breaking up with Pearce. I told him I was raped by JJ. Instead of standing by me, Pearce blames me. I am so stressed out from crying. I have lost so much weight. I have no energy. I don't know how to keep functioning in my life."

"Is Pearce moving out of your house?"

"For months, Pearce and I have been fighting about this. Sometimes he is moving out and then he decides to stay. I try to work things out with him but he is so infuriated with me."

"Why is he angry?"

"He disapproves of everything I do. He tells me he can't keep up with my spending. My mother bought me a young horse because my stallion is getting very old. I now have three horses and a pony to feed. I also have my dogs, cats and goats. Pearce wants me to sell my animals."

"Can you afford to feed all your animals?"

"I am earning money as a belly dancer. I have been dancing at restaurants and for parties and art gallery openings. You see, making money and saving money is not my life's goal. Spending money on things I love makes me happy. I use money for happiness. I won't sacrifice what I love just so I have money. I won't sell my animals just to save money."

"Do you still love Pearce?"

"Yes, but I am sick of his disapproval. He tells me he won't be a partner to me while I mismanage my assets. His words. Honestly, he is a beautiful man but his opinionated, judgmental, uncompassionate and intolerant ways of looking at life turn me off."

"What is JJ doing? Is he remorseful for what he did to you?"

"JJ is horrible to me. He tells me that suffering is good for me and he wants to make me suffer. He expects me to marry him but when I refuse, he threatens me. He is loaded on all sorts of drugs all the time. I am sick of JJ's drugs! He is not a beautiful man. He has gained a lot of weight as he eats too much junk. He has a destructive lifestyle."

"Do you love JJ?"

"I used to love him dearly when I first met him when I was nineteen. Sometimes, I see a glimmer of his kind heart. He asks me why things didn't work out between Pearce and I. I tell JJ that I was forced to tell Pearce that JJ raped me. I never wanted to tell Pearce but JJ threatened to kill Pearce. JJ thinks Pearce doesn't love me enough. JJ thinks Pearce is using me and just wants to claim my land and my ranch."

"What do you want to do with your life now?"

"I think I should get rid of both of these men."

"Is there any hope for Pearce in the future?"

"Maybe he could come back to me when he can truly appreciate me. He needs better opportunities with his music career. He is unhappy in Santo and he takes his frustrations out on me. Pearce hates JJ. He doesn't trust me. I want him to move out now. Maybe he will miss me. It would be nice if Pearce valued me like he used to when we first fell in love."

"Is there hope for JJ?"

"I want JJ to go into rehab. If he doesn't, he will do an overdose and die. JJ is jealous of Pearce. He is trying to frighten Pearce to get him out of my life. JJ thinks once Pearce is gone, JJ can force me to marry him. I tell JJ that I won't marry a drug addict but he won't listen to me. He has no respect for me at all. He is getting what he wants by having Pearce move out. This might pacify him until I can get him into rehab."

"Can I share something with you?"

"Please. I need insight."

"In the beginning of my relationship with my husband, before we got married, I discovered that he was cheating on me. We broke up. Two years later, I saw him at a business function and we started dating again. We got married. We have been happily married now for fifteen years. We have a beautiful daughter together. Toni, you just never know how your life will turn out." She smiles sweetly.

"Thank you for telling me this story. It takes years for love to formulate, doesn't it? Your marriage is a good example."

"How is your young horse doing? My daughter has been begging me for a horse since she was ten-years-old. Now she is thirteen and she just started taking riding lessons. I have become very fond of horses."

"Kamar is spooky and he frightens me. He likes to rear up suddenly if he hears a strange noise or if he sees a sudden movement. I am riding him but when he gets too excited, I jump off and walk him until he calms down. He chews continuously on his bit, he dislikes spurs and he hates the crop I use to encourage him to behave. I also use a tie-down to keep him from rearing too high. Every time he rears, he loses his balance and falls over backwards."

"Is he worth keeping if he is dangerous to ride?"

"I am not giving up on Kamar. I keep riding him as often as I can. He needs a lot of attention. And he is a lot better to ride when I ride him with someone else riding Silvano, my other Arabian horse."

"Well, don't forget to wear your helmet!" she warns.

ↄ

Pearce is moving his guitars and amplifiers out of my studio. He is moving to a friend's house in Santo.

"You seem happy that I'm moving, Toni."

"I love your body, Pearce. But I don't like what you do or how you think. You are too conservative and rigid in your thinking now. I am tired of being with a musician. It's not romantic anymore. You forbid me to come to your gigs and you won't involve me with your music world. You lose your temper if I even talk to the singer of your band. The only thing we have in common is our sexual attraction for each other. And even this is wearing thin from your constant criticism of me and my life."

"You always claimed to love me more than I love you."

"This is true. You are the one who is intolerant. Intolerance is not love. When I met you, people warned me not to get involved with you. They said you were a drunk and a womanizer...a real wolf. And you've always had Sheila in your life, bringing you lunch, taking you to fancy dinners and buying you memberships to expensive health clubs. You even prefer to ride her horses with her than with me on mine. She flies you to places with her on her private jet. You spend time with her that I don't even know about. I have been very tolerant of all this. I trust what you need to do with your life. I am jealous of Sheila's money but I accept Sheila in your life because I love you. Your ultimatums are not love. Yes, I have always loved you more than you love me."

"I'm leaving you because of JJ."

"I told you about JJ when we first met years ago. You asked me not to talk about him. You told me I could do what I wanted as long as it didn't involve you. And after telling me this, you now accuse me of being dishonest. I was respecting your wishes though. I felt I needed to protect you and tell you about JJ as now it did involve you. You are angry if I talk about him and you are angry if I don't talk about him. I can't win with you. You demand that I never see JJ again. I can't do this. I am afraid that he will kill me if I tell him this. I need to protect my life even if you refuse to protect me. My only safety is to get JJ into rehab. You are leaving. It's your choice. The truth is you don't want to be with me. I accept this. I let you go. I have seen your interior iciness so I am glad you are leaving. The only reason I would want you to stay is to protect me from JJ."

"I want to be in an environment where I am in no danger from JJ."

"You are more interested in protecting yourself than in protecting me. Some man you are! And you claim to love me?"

"I can't support your lifestyle. I can't support your animals."

"Then go and support yourself. You'll be happier. If you loved me, you would protect me from JJ. If you loved me, you wouldn't leave me. You would help me keep JJ away and encourage me to get JJ into rehab. You would stand by me, come what may. You don't love me anymore. I see you for what you are now. You have failed my test of love. I need a man to offer his support and his approval. You don't enjoy spending time with me anymore. You don't give me any of your attention anymore."

"Well, I am not going to waste any time seeing you once I move out!"

I had lent Pearce some of my furniture to use in my studio. As he packs, I begin to move my furniture back into my house. While he carries his belongings into a borrowed van parked in front of the studio, I pick up my very heavy desk. I almost drop it. Pearce comes over and grabs it.

"You are so stupid, Toni, I have my own moving to do. I don't want to help you move too."

"Anyone who talks to me like this is not my friend!"

"You have ruined my life."

"You can't offer love to anyone as you are too miserable with yourself. Don't blame me. Concentrate on making yourself happy and then maybe you will have something to give someone else. I don't need your help. You are free to go to Chicago and pursue your music career. You have no responsibilities or things to tie you down now."

"The only way I would be happy with you again is if you obeyed me."

"You are a tyrant."

"I am not. Tyrants are destructive."

"You are killing emotions!"

"I am happier without you. I don't want to see you anymore. I am doing you a favor by leaving you. Once you pay off your mortgage in a year, you will be making income from the studio. Then you will be able to support your animals."

"You are right. My bills stress you out. Now you don't have to feel responsible for my spending. You value your career more than you value me. I want a man who can take me camping in the wilderness with my horses. You don't even like country living! You will be happier living in the city."

༄

JJ has just arrived, loaded and crazy. He goes directly to the corral and gets my wheelbarrow and shovel. Then he starts shoveling manure from the compost pile into the wheelbarrow. I watch him as he pushes the wheelbarrow to my garden.

"JJ, you don't need to do this."

"I want to help you with your garden. I want to move into your empty studio. This is a way I can show you how I can help around your ranch."

"I rented my studio out yesterday, JJ."

"What? Who to?"

"A website designer named Ned and his ten-year-old daughter, Karen. They both love animals. Karen held Creamy Snowflake and Ned played with my old dog Kira. Kira doesn't like many people so I think Ned will work out. I feel comfortable with them living next door."

Kira is a white and fluffy American Eskimo dog. Her first owners bred American Eskimo dogs. Kira had complications during the delivery of her last litter of puppies. Her puppies were stillborn and to save Kira's life, she was spaid. The owners could no longer use her for breeding so they put an ad in the newspaper, looking for a good home for her. My father had just died when I saw the ad. I was having difficulty understanding and accepting my father's death. I called the owners and they told me where they lived so I got in my little truck to get her.

I was at a stoplight in the far left-hand lane of a three-lane highway when I looked in my rear-view mirror. A black van was racing toward the parked cars to my right. The van didn't stop. The earsplitting sound of crunching metal and skidding tires will never leave my memory. Without thinking, I drove into the concrete isle to my left just in time to avoid the nine-car pile-up behind me. Shaking to my core, I turned around and drove home. On the evening news, I saw the dreadful accident from a helicopter's perspective. The driver of the black van was killed instantly. He was intoxicated.

Thankfully, Kira's owners brought Kira to me. She was traumatized from losing her litter of puppies. I was in shock from witnessing that terrible car accident. We bonded immediately. Kira has brought me comfort and healing for years.

"You promised me you'd rent your studio to me."

"I will never rent to a junkie. Don't delude yourself. Putting manure on my garden is not helping me. A long time ago, my mother asked you to be concerned about my welfare with no strings attached. Apparently, you help me with a huge string of attachment. You want marriage. Well, I won't marry you. I will never marry a drug addict. You hang around your low-life friends that use drugs, get drunk and hurt all the people around them. When you are high, I am afraid for my life. You destroy yourself and everyone around you. You are sick and you need help. Until you go into rehab, there is nothing decent about you. You are not helping me unless you can be kind and sensitive. Do not come near me again until you are sober. If you try to hurt me again, I will call the police."

"I will get my Hell's Angel friends to come and beat you up."

"I will protect myself."

"I've worked hard for you all these years, Toni."

"You've worked hard for all your buddies and your crack whores, not me. You've never given me what you promised me. Three years ago, you promised to buy me a big truck so I could pull my horse trailer. There is no sign of a truck. You aren't the person I once knew."

"I want to back out of your life then.""

"Good. I don't want you to bring danger into my life anymore."

"Well, what can I do to bring you and Pearce back together?"

"It's too late. You've already destroyed my relationship with Pearce. I'm on my own now."

"I've loved you all these years, Toni."

"No, you are selfish and immature. You can't think of anyone but yourself. You just want to marry me and ruin my life to get what you want. I have never been so unhappy. I can hardly eat. I am suffering from anorexia and serious trauma from the sex you forced on me. A man doesn't rape someone he loves. He doesn't threaten to kill a woman he loves."

"But I do love you whether you believe me or not."

"I'm sorry, JJ. Men don't know how to love me. They just want to take away my inner light, my vitality and my energy. And you, more than all the men in my past, have betrayed me the most. Why? I have known you the longest. I believed in your good heart. If I can get away from negative forces like you, I can begin to eat again. I need to stop trusting men like you. Evil surrounds you. You need my energy to suck on like a vampire since your natural energy is dead, killed by all the chemicals you feed yourself every day. You are a spiritual parasite! You create foul psychic atmosphere around you. I need to clean my world of your bad energy. You are out-of-control, spinning counterclockwise, downward to Hell on earth. No amount of money can compensate for the psychological damage you have done to me."

"You are talking crazy. It sounds like you are the one for the nuthouse. Would you like me to commit you? Do you need a place where you can rest and learn to eat normally again? I will pay for this if you need it."

"You would love to have me locked up, wouldn't you? You are the one that needs to be locked up. You are dominated by the devil of your own making. You need to be exorcised and you need rehab!"

❧

I have driven into Santo to have another session with Mrs. Yender. What a relief it is to collapse in her comfortable couch.

"Toni, I am worried about you. You have lost more weight since our last meeting."

"I am scared to death of JJ. And now Pearce is gone without a backward glance. My only friends are my animals. I don't know how I could survive without their love and emotional support. My mother wants to help me but all she can tell me is to be strong. How can I be strong?"

"First of all, JJ knows that you care about him and this is what pulls him to you. If you truly didn't care about JJ, he'd stop calling and visiting you. Your troubles arise from your need to give to people who never give back. You wish people would reciprocate but all they do is abuse you. You must learn how to demand that people give to you or you are not interested in them. Don't let anyone touch you who doesn't give back, who doesn't bring you happiness and comfort. And, Toni, you are not JJ's salvation. Don't reject him because then he will hurt you or kill you. Your instincts are right about him even if Pearce will never believe how right you are in protecting your life. And you no longer need to be JJ's angel of goodness and his object of desire. You need to learn how to be totally indifferent to JJ. Don't put any energy into him. Don't give him any of your thoughts or feelings.

You can lose Pearce but you cannot lose your own inner power. Let people like Pearce go. You do not need friends who treat you badly. Do not diminish your power for anyone. Don't let your beautiful qualities of compassion and goodness be stomped on by people who do not recognize you.

Don't give yourself away, to anyone. Demand your due, Toni. Don't provide nourishment for the blood-suckers of the world. If you let people abuse you, they will hate you and spit on you all the more. Don't be a poor weak creature when you really are such a kind, generous and loving spirit. Outlaw people who do not treat you like the queen of goodness that you are.

You can't eat and sleep because you are tortured beyond endurance by the lack of tenderness in both Pearce and JJ. You need to have nothing to offer Pearce or JJ. They abuse you with their lack of tenderness. You are losing your power. By losing your power, you betray yourself and you bring out the worst in people because they know they can get away with mistreating you. Do yourself and everyone around you a favor: refuse to be damaged or injured any longer. Claim your power! You may feel too afraid to recognize this now but you have powers that other people need to be afraid of. You have the right to claim yourself as Queen! I am asking you to only spend time with people as long as they treat you like the Queen you truly are. Can you promise me this?"

"I can try." I am crying softly. I let my guard down when I am relaxed in Mrs. Yender's brown couch. I know she is telling me the truth and I trust her. She may be the only person in the world that I can trust. I know she wants only what is good for me, with no personal gain for herself involved. She doesn't even charge me her full price for our sessions as she knows I make very little money as a dancer.

"I have been offered a full-time job as a secretary at a real estate agency. Now that I am on my own without support from Pearce or JJ, I need to figure out a way to support my animals myself. Do you think I should accept this job offer?"

"Toni, you are in no condition physically or emotionally to work at a full-time job. As a secretary, the demands on you will be constant. You need to focus on regaining your own inner and outer strength back after last month's life-threatening rape and then your horrible break-up with Pearce. JJ is hounding and harassing you. Your plate is full. A full-time job will only cause you to go over your edge. I am worried that the exterior pressure will ultimately cause you to have a nervous breakdown or a physical illness. Your body is too thin. You need to focus on nourishing your body and not putting anymore demands on it than you already have."

"Yesterday, my brother Brant drove over to my house in his four-wheel drive jeep. He hooked it to my horse trailer. I am so excited. We loaded both my horses into the horse trailer for the first time. We drove the trailer with the horses up my road and back as a test run. We want to go camping with the horses. This has been my dream for over five years. Our only problem is that Brant's jeep is old and deteriorating. I know this may sound silly, but I need to buy a truck strong enough to pull my trailer. JJ has been promising to buy me one but he always breaks his promises. How am I ever going to afford a truck unless I get a full-time job?"

"You need to cut all ties with JJ. This is true. But as much as you need a big truck, what about taking care of your tiny, disappearing body, Toni?"

"Manifesting a truck and taking my horses camping will give me the desire to eat and the will to want to be healthy again. I need that truck as incentive for me to look forward to my future. Right now, I am buried in the torture of my life."

"I see your point, Toni. You need something to look forward to. Well, if it's a truck that makes you want to be healthy and you feel this new job will bring enthusiasm and energy in your life, then I say give it a try. I cannot stop you from trying. I must say, you are the only person I know whose thread of life-support is connected to a truck," she says, laughing.

☙

It is six in the morning and I have to be at work in two hours to open the real estate office. I only have one hour to ride Kamar but my goal is to ride him before I go to work every morning. I dress quickly, pulling on my jeans, t-shirt and white cowboy boots. I slide my black riding helmet over my head and clasp its latches securely under my chin.

It is a beautiful, warm July morning. Kamar greets me with energetic, friendly nibbles. He willingly lets me saddle him. He has always hated the Tom Thumb bit but I feel I need the extra control so I slip it into his mouth. He begins to chomp away at it, which is normal for him. I jump into his saddle and we ride out of the corral. We pass my horse trailer in the yard. Brant left his jeep hooked up to my trailer so we can practice loading the horses into the trailer when he comes over to visit.

Kamar and I start up a wide arroyo. I let Kamar canter but I try to keep him from running too fast in case he spooks and I lose all control of him. We walk up a ridge. I get off and I hug my young Arabian horse with great affection. How I love this horse! We gaze at the pink mesas and the distant blue mountains in the morning light. I always feel such joy when I am in harmony with Kamar. I only want more unison between us in the future. I get back into the saddle and I think to myself how Kamar is being especially compliant this morning. I have earned this. I have worked hard to learn how to ride this horse.

I decide to ride the dirt road home. I have been riding this dirt road since I was nine-years-old on my first Shetland pony. Today I am distracted by my thoughts. I must get home by seven. I don't notice the chipped gravel newly piled on top of the dirt road. Later, I find out that the county of Santo put chipped gravel on the road the day before. As Kamar walks on the gravel, it shifts around under his horseshoes. I notice a jogger running behind us. I pet Kamar, reassuring him that the jogger won't hurt him. The jogger smiles at me as he runs past us. I smile back. Without warning, Kamar is down, sliding in the gravel on his knees. I manage to pull his head up. He scrambles to his feet only to collapse to the ground. I am thrown to the gravel. My head hits the road. My helmet protects my head but I see that Kamar is seriously injured. Deep red blood is gushing from both his knees. If I am going to save his life, I must get help. I act rapidly.

"Help me! Help me!" I scream. The jogger hears me. He sees that my horse is down on the ground. He runs back to me.

"Oh my God! What happened?" he asks.

"My horse just fell and slid on his knees on this gravel. I need you to watch him while I go get help."

"Of course. Go!"

Luckily, a man driving a car is approaching us. I wave him down and he gives me a ride to my house. I call my sister.

"Annie, I need you to call Villa Vet. I just had a serious accident with my horse Kamar up the road. I need to go back and be with my horse but I need you to call Villa Vet's emergency number. They are closed now but leave a message with your phone number so they can call you back. Tell them I am on the road above my house. They know where I live. The vets have been out to my house before. I don't have time to sit and call and wait for an answer. I need to go back to Kamar. He might die! I have never seen so much blood. Please, help me."

"I can't. I am on my way to school. I don't have time."

"This is an emergency! My horse is bleeding to death!" I am furious with my sister. She always pretends to be my friend but when I really need her help, she seems to enjoy disappointing me. I hang up the phone. I run as fast as I can to a neighbor's house. I wildly bang on the door.

"What the hell is wrong?" asks an American Indian who opens his old wooden door.

"Please help me. I need you to call Villa Vet and leave your number." I explain my plan to this startled Indian. He agrees to call Villa Vet and wait for their return call. He even agrees to give them directions to my suffering horse.

"Wait a minute," he says. He runs into a back room in his house and returns with large strips of a sheet he has just torn up.

"Here. Use these to wrap your horse's knees. It will stop the flow of blood."

"Thank you, thank you." I grab the sheet strips and run back to my house. I jump into Brant's jeep. The keys are in the ignition. I am so grateful that the jeep and my horse trailer are already attached. What a blessing! I drive the jeep and horse trailer back up to Kamar. I need to get Kamar to Villa Vet so the vets can save his life!

A group of five men have gathered around Kamar who is laying on the road. These men are neighbors that heard my screams as well as men who were driving by and stopped to see if they could help. There is nothing as heart-breaking as a beautiful, proud horse dying on the ground. I back up the trailer so it is near Kamar. I park the jeep and trailer, jump out and fall to my knees where my beloved horse lies. Kamar's eyes are closed.

"Oh no!" I yell. I touch Kamar's nose. He is still breathing. I gently lift his shredded knees and I wrap the strips of fabric around and around each of his bloody knees. The white cloth immediately turns crimson. I weep hysterically. The men around me watch helplessly as I break down in front of them.

"Kamar. Please don't die. Don't die. Don't die." I chant these two words, over and over. My breath is now convulsions of uncontrollable sobs. I ask the men to please stay and help me. I tell them that a vet is on his way and I will need them to help me to lift my horse into my trailer. The men nod their heads in unison. I don't even know these men or their names and they want to help me. I look at them with a solemn smile of deep gratitude. They understand my distress.

Trent from Villa Vet arrives. Trent pulled out a bad tooth Kamar had recently so he knows Kamar. Trent immediately injects a pain killer into Kamar's neck. Trent then gets a rope and with the help of the five men, he lifts my crippled horse into the trailer. It is a miracle that I had so many men to help the vet. I thank the men for helping me and my poor horse. I quickly start driving the ten miles to Villa Vet with Trent following closely in his truck.

I know that I am going to lose my new job but I don't care. My therapist warned me not to take this job. Suddenly the engine in Brant's jeep is making terrible sounds. It clatters as if it will blow up. I can't get out of second gear so I drive in second gear for the entire ten miles to Villa Vet. I need my own truck!

I pull into the Villa Vet driveway and Trent tells his assistant what to do. The other vets gather to help unload Kamar onto a platform with wheels and cart him to the hospital room. There is nothing more I can do.

"Trent, please save Kamar's life."

"Toni, from what I have seen, it doesn't look good. Both his knees are crushed to the bone. If he broke the bones, he will be in serious pain. He may not survive from all the blood loss. I may have to put him down. Are you prepared to do this?"

"No. No, I won't let Kamar die. He can't die. I love him too much."

"Well, I will do my best. But this will be very expensive. How do you plan to pay for this?"

"I will find the money, don't you worry. Just take care of Kamar. I will be home waiting for your call. Please call me as soon as you know something."

જી

"Kamar has had a serious accident. I need your help!" I have just returned home and decide to call JJ.

"What happened?"

"Kamar fell this morning around seven as I was riding home. He is now in a vet hospital. Can you please help me pay his vet bills?"

"You only call me when you need money."

"Did you hear me, JJ? I had a serious accident this morning with Kamar! Is this all you can say to me?"

"You love your horses more than you love me, Toni. When I ask you if I can move into your studio so you can nurse me back to health, you refuse. So why should I help you nurse your horse?"

"You have no compassion. I need comfort and all you can think about is your poor pitiful self. My horse might die and all you care about is your stupid money."

"If you need money, why don't you mortgage your land?"

"I already have a mortgage on my land."

"Well, you said I wasn't welcome on your land. So why should I help you? You don't even love me. You won't marry me."

"I just want you to go into rehab and get straight, JJ. You have been promising me to do this for years. I lost my job today when I didn't go to work. I have a beautiful horse in terrible pain in the hospital. I just thought you'd have enough heart to care. Well, you don't. I will never call you again."

ꙮ

"Mother, can you help me?"

"I heard from your sister that you had an accident with Kamar. Are you hurt?"

"No, mother. The helmet I was wearing protected my head when I fell to the ground on Kamar. I am just very upset because I need to find a way to pay Kamar's vet bills. All I care about is Kamar. I need to save his life. When I didn't go to work today, I received a phone message that I was fired. I just called JJ and asked if he would help and he refused. I need you, mother. Can you help me at all?"

"Of course, Toni. We will pay the vet with a credit card I use only for emergencies. Please don't call JJ again. He says he loves you but he really doesn't care about you or your horse. What is important now is helping Kamar."

"Thank you, mother. Thank you so much! You are always there for me when I need you the most. I love you so much! I wish I had never taken the secretarial job. Then I wouldn't have been riding Kamar so early this morning. I wish I could change events. I just want my horse back. Oh mother, I need a miracle!"

"The job wasn't right for you anyway. You are a dancer, not a secretary. And now you will need time to take care of Kamar. I am sure the vets at Villa Vet will save his life. But he will be lame for a very long time. You will need to be his nurse. I worry about how thin you have gotten. You need time to take care of yourself properly so you have the stamina to take good care of Kamar."

"Oh mother. I need to stay away from all hateful people. I need to learn how to become self-sufficient. I need to be more careful. I need time to nurture myself and my animals. And I need Kamar to survive!"

ꙮ

"As you know, Kamar sustained severe damage to both his knees in his fall the other day. The damage to his right knee is more extensive than to his left knee. In radiographs I took of the right knee, there is evidence of damage to the bones in the lower part of the joint. These bones were ground down by the gravel road. On radiographs I took of the left knee, there is similar damage. There will be callus formation or bony growth at the injury sight. This could cause Kamar to be lame. The prognosis for Kamar's future soundness is guarded, Toni."

I am talking with Trent at Villa Vet. Brant is here with me, listening silently. We brought Brant's jeep and my horse trailer to bring Kamar home. Kamar has been hospitalized for two days.

"I have done everything I can do. I encourage you to put Kamar down. He may never walk again. You will never ride him again."

"I cannot allow you to put my beautiful colt to sleep. I cannot. I want to bring my colt home and take care of him myself. What do I need to do?" I ask sadly.

"Kamar should get Gentocin injections once a day in the morning and penicillin injections every morning and evening for the next three days. On the fourth day, Kamar needs thirty trimethoprim-sulfa antibiotic tablets every day, fifteen in the morning and fifteen in the evening. These pills can be fed in wet grain or given as a paste by dissolving them in water in a syringe. He also needs one gram of bute paste orally twice a day for the next week. This is for the extreme pain he is in now. After a week, give Kamar bute paste as needed."

"How do I bandage Kamar's knees?" I ask. I hope I don't sound as alarmed as I feel.

"You will need to change the bandages on both knees daily. When you change the bandages, remove the old one and gently clean the wounds on both knees with mild soap, water and a wash cloth. For the first four days, hose above and below the wounds for fifteen minutes on each knee with cold water while the bandages are off. Allow the knees about twenty minutes to air dry. Apply Furozone, this antibiotic ointment I have here, to gauze squares. Put the squares directly on to the wounds. Wrap his knees with bandages and cover these with polo wrap. Keep the wraps securely on his knees with black electrical tape.

You will do this every day until the drainage from the open joints stops. This could be up to two weeks. After this, you can change the bandages every two days until the wounds are filled in and even with his skin. After this, Kamar's knees can be healed open to the air."

"Okay. Where should I keep him?"

"He should be confined to a small stall for the next month during the initial healing stage. After the first two weeks, you can try to walk him around for ten minutes a day. I would like to see him in two weeks to evaluate his progress. And Toni, you can always feel free to call me if you have any problems or questions."

I am overwhelmed with the labor-intensive responsibility ahead of me but I am determined to save Kamar's life. Brant and I load Kamar easily into my trailer and when we arrive at my ranch, I am so glad that my little colt is home! I put Kamar in Khalifah's stall. I put Silvano in the stall next to Kamar to keep Kamar company. I put Khalifah and his mare in corrals over the hill from my house.

Now I have to give Kamar his evening injections. I am needle phobic. I dislike giving and receiving injections immensely. I have to be brave. Brant stands by me as I inject Kamar's neck with the needle. I have to draw all my inner resources together to heal Kamar. I have to focus on my love for Kamar and visualize him healed, healthy and walking again!

♋

"Mother, how can you be so positive? How can I visualize his knees back to normal when they look so terrible now?" My mother is helping me change Kamar's bandages. It is not easy to do this by myself. The bandages come undone easily especially when Kamar grabs them off with his teeth. I have learned that I need to cover the bandages tightly with the polo wraps.

"Toni, as long as you keep negative people away, you can stay happy in your inner world. Negative people only have control over you if you fear them. If you remain happy, their negativity will fizzle out eventually. The secret to being positive is to do things that make you feel happy. Taking care of Kamar is a wonderful thing to do. Not listening to negativity is the best thing you can do. Don't listen to the vets who tell you that Kamar will never walk again. Remember how much you loved riding Kamar before his accident? You will ride Kamar again as long as you focus on the happiness in your life."

"I am getting phone messages from JJ again. He keeps saying that he loves me in the messages. How can he love me? He won't help me with Kamar's vet bills. You are the only one helping me."

"You know that I love you very much and I will do anything I can to help you. I am proud of all your many accomplishments."

"Thank you. I am trying so hard. I am praying that Kamar walks again. I have to give him painkillers every day and I don't like the fact that he is in so much pain. My friend Jane tells me that I am inhumane not to allow the vet to put Kamar to sleep. She says that putting Kamar down is an act of mercy and kindness. How can this be?"

When my mother ponders a question, she has a habit of reaching her left hand up to twist her shoulder length golden-brown hair with her slim fingers. Her light blue eyes study me.

"Look at Kamar, Toni. If Kamar wanted to die, his eyes wouldn't be bright and curious. His ears wouldn't be forward. Kamar wants to live. It will be difficult work for you for a long time but nature heals. Trust your heart. I believe what Joseph Campbell says: 'Follow your bliss.' Kamar is worth saving. He is a young colt. He wants your love. And you love him enough to save him. Give Mother Nature a chance to heal Kamar now. Mother Nature can work wonders.

When I was a teenager, I broke my back. I was riding a wild horse in a rodeo and this horse threw me off. I spent an entire summer on my back not knowing if I would ever walk again. At that time, the doctors couldn't do anything for a broken back. Nature worked her miracles and slowly I recovered. Nature helped me when the doctors couldn't. You have to trust Mother Nature now."

I stare deeply into Kamar's brown eyes. Mother is right. Kamar may be in pain but he still has interest in his surroundings. His ears are alert, moving back and forth, listening to our words. Kamar is not laying down to die. He has a determination to live.

"In one of the messages I received from JJ yesterday, he said he needed a heart transplant. Is he just going insane? He needs to get off the drugs. No one he knows is willing to intervene. I called JJ's parents. His father told me he has given up on JJ. I told his father that I would still help JJ if he went into rehab. His father knows that JJ's violence scares me to death."

"You shouldn't have to cope with JJ's drug-induced rage and insanity. Focus on your injured colt now. Kamar needs you more than anyone. JJ doesn't need you. He manipulates you to try to keep you in his vile life. Keep your attention on healing Kamar. What you focus on expands. What you ignore goes away. Put all your energy and positive thinking on your beautiful colt and watch the dark clouds disappear out of your life. You are my precious daughter, my wild flower and my bright star. I admire you. I only want the best for you, always."

I look at my wounded colt and I say a silent prayer: "Please Mother Nature, please heal Kamar's knees! Please let him walk again perfectly!"

❧

"Joy, thank you for coming over to see Kamar!" Joy is a neighbor and we ride our horses together occasionally. Joy loves to ride bareback. Her passion is her mare and the mare's filly that Joy is training herself. Her short brown hair frames her sweet, chubby face.

"I brought something for you to put in Kamar's barn. It is a plaque to the Virgin Mary. In Mexico, the Virgin Mary is a goddess and a saint. She will heal Kamar."

"You are so thoughtful. All I want is my colt's knees to heal. This is my biggest goal. Anything else is minor compared to this. I want my colt back! My greatest happiness now is helping my colt to heal. It is difficult to keep Kamar's bandages on. When they slide off, lots of flies get on his wounds. I panic because Trent at Villa Vet warns me that Kamar's injuries are very serious and I must keep his knees bandaged. So, I started bandaging Kamar's knees with duct tape.

David, another vet at Villa Vet, is more positive. He said supplements for Kamar are good. He said ligament fiber can be regenerated. He told me that my elbow grease is the best thing I have. He means that if I do all the work, Kamar will heal. He encourages me to do Kamar's physical therapy once the bandages come off. I told David that when I stop giving Kamar bute for a day, Kamar gets worse and he cannot put weight on his right leg. I don't like giving Kamar drugs every day but David told me that Kamar needs bute for a long time as Kamar is in a lot of pain. He said Kamar's front ligaments are torn in half. Until Kamar regenerates new ligament, he shouldn't move. Oh Joy! When my friend Jane visits me, she seems certain that Kamar will never walk again. I am in tears after I talk to her."

"Toni, concentrate on peace and healing for Kamar. You need a miracle. Accidents happen so we can witness miracles. You need to visualize Kamar's knees healed. Why don't you call the horse vets in Santo who heal in an alternative way? Go on the Internet and find out ways to heal horses with problems like Kamar. Ask Tierra, the spirit of the land, to help you. If you remain calm and hopeful, the land can give you power. Kamar depends on you to be filled with faith even when other people are doubtful. Stay away from fear and hopelessness. Your mantra needs to be 'faith, peace, calm, power.'

Also, make a clay replica of Kamar with perfect knees. Put healing herbs in the clay. When the clay dries, put this clay horse in a special place where you can see it daily. This will give you confidence."

"I'll put this Virgin Mary plaque here in Kamar's barn. Joy, you are such an amazing woman. Thank you for all your emotional support and practical and spiritual suggestions. I will do them all. I need my time now to devote to Kamar. My mission is to get him to walk around without pain. I don't have time to date men anymore. Dating seems ridiculous and most men seem shallow. Dating feels very superficial compared to the hours I spend every day healing Kamar. His injuries force me to stay resolute. I need inner peace no matter what is going on around me."

⁊

Trent has arrived to evaluate Kamar's progress. Trent listens to my doubts. I don't like to tell him about my concerns as I know he tends to be very negative.

"I am worried because Kamar can't put weight on his right leg, Trent."

"You are doing a good job keeping Kamar's knees clean. The left knee already has tissue over the bone. The right knee is healing slower; the bone on this knee is still exposed. Continue changing the bandages on the right knee every day with Furozone. Change the bandage on the left knee every two days now, with caustic powder on top of the Furozone. When the bandages are off, use water massage for five minutes above and five minutes below the wounds on both knees. And continue to give Kamar one gram of bute once a day."

"I went on the Internet and I got some alternative healing suggestions from vets from other equine clinics. What do you think of Calendula gel to promote healing? And the homeopathic treatment of Arnica for pain? The homeopathic treatment of Ruta Grav was suggested to me to help heal Kamar's ligaments. Magnetic wraps can help increase blood flow to the injured area which also promotes healing. What do you think, Trent?"

"Those alternative treatments cannot hurt Kamar. I would like you to start a daily routine of hand walking Kamar for five to ten minutes. We have to exercise him a little so he doesn't get colic. Feed him a little bran. Stop feeding him grain and alfalfa. Timothy grass hay is fine. Kamar also needs probiotics to replace the flora in his intestines."

"All right. Thank you for coming over." When Trent writes my bill, I am surprised at the high charge for the farm visit. I am using my mother's credit card for Kamar's expenses. I have promised my mother that I will pay her back. I am keeping track of my costs. I have spent almost fifteen hundred dollars so far and I know the expenses are just starting.

I get my water massager and start to spray water above and below the wounds on Kamar's knees. He tosses his head up and acts like he might rear. This little gesture gives my heart a jolt of hope! This is the first sign that Kamar's true personality is returning. He will be very wild in a year but I just want my colt back. I could get another horse if Kamar can't be ridden again. I love Kamar and I will keep him as a pet no matter what happens. I will work hard at healing Kamar's knees as he deserves a chance.

I have found a lawyer named Jim Apples who has agreed to represent me against the Santo County. He doesn't think I will win a case like this as he tells me that horses have no rights in this state. But he has agreed to make a complaint. I need to at least make a claim and report Kamar's injuries. All my friends want to vouch for my safe riding skills. I have received letters of recommendation from Joy, Jane, Brant and Pearce. Joy's husband did not want Joy to get involved but Joy wants to help me as she is my riding buddy. Even if the County does nothing, I will feel better for trying. It hurts me deeply to watch how Kamar can hardly step forward without pain.

Pearce's letter of recommendation touches me profoundly:

Dear Sirs: Toni is the most meticulous horse person I have ever known. She started riding and caring for horses when she was ten years old. To my knowledge, she has never had any type of accident with horses. She spares no expense on training, equipment, nutrition and safety. Her little horse, Kamar, was her pride and joy. She spent all her time possible with that horse. She had a good trainer and always wore her helmet as safety was her first concern. Toni was raised on the same ranch she lives on now and has been riding around that area all her life. She knows the area better than anyone. The county road out to her ranch has always been a dirt-packed road. Suddenly the county came and dumped sharp chipped and slippery gravel on this road. The chipped gravel is most certainly responsible for causing Kamar to stumble. Kamar was a very sure-footed horse. All the times I rode him or rode along with him, I have never seen him trip, fall or stumble. Kamar just couldn't stay up on that gravel and it is necessary to cross that county road to get in and out of Toni's ranch. When the horse slipped, the gravel tore through his skin and severed the ligaments of his knees.

Kamar may never walk again and will possibly never be able to be ridden again. He is only five years old and he had a bright and happy future. He was a talented and intelligent horse and would have gone a long way with Toni. For Toni, this tragedy is beyond heartbreaking. She has been devastated by this. She was forced to quit her promising new job and almost all her other activities as the horse requires near constant care with painkillers, antibiotics, water massage and bandaging on a daily basis. All this plus vet bills and huge expenses in trying every possible way to save her horse's legs have placed an enormous financial burden on Toni. I have been riding with Toni for many years and I am certain none of this would have ever happened if it weren't for that sharp gravel the county poured all over the county road.

I want Pearce to know how I feel so I write him a letter in response:

Dear Pearce: I love and adore you and I always will. I don't live my life to hurt you. I live my life to grow and discover what shoes fit me and what I resonate with. I am looking for my niche in life. I try shoes on and then I find out they don't fit. So, I take them off and discard them. When JJ makes me feel worse, I discard him. If you don't like coming out to my ranch and if you don't like spending time with my animals, injured or well, then I can't feel close to you anymore. My animals are my entire life. They keep me alive. Their love is consistent and pure. They love me no matter what shoes I am experimenting with. I wish your love was as consistent. Your disapproval of me hurts me so much that I get depressed. It's better that either you accept me, love me and help me with love in your heart or I stop seeing you until I can straighten my life out to your approval. The thing is, I may never please you. You may lose me permanently. Without your love and guidance, I feel weak and vulnerable. I need to feel loved. Your angry control of me does not make me feel loved. It makes me want to run away from you. If you want to help me, you need to be a guiding light not a controlling combatant. I need your gentle love. Please don't let your anger drive me away from you. Don't throw me to the dragons. Keep me wanting to love you. Keep me desiring to be near you. You can keep me only with your loving support. I am begging you to love the parts of me that you do like. Be patient as I fumble along in life trying to fix my deep wounds. I need support while I fix Kamar's wounds too. I feel very helpless. I need your help. Help me with your patience, love and tolerance. I am trying to heal parts of me as I try to heal Kamar.

౭౩

Joy has just ridden her mare over to my ranch to check on Kamar.

"Joy, I am so relieved to show you how Kamar is beginning to walk a little. He is still very stiff at first. I walk him a little further each day. His knees get better when he moves around more. Yesterday, I was able to walk him to the big corral over the hill. He is still very frustrated that he cannot move very quickly. He bit my left middle finger so hard that I think the nail might come off."

"His knees are looking so much better. What are you doing to heal him now?"

"I have stopped bandaging with polo-wraps on his knees. I use magnet wraps now. I think magnets will help heal Kamar's bones and torn ligaments."

"You look so much happier now, Toni," she says smiling. I can feel her genuine concern for me and my horse.

"I am so grateful to Mr. Apples, my lawyer. He sent off a Tort Claim to Santo County, describing how Kamar was seriously injured in the fall on the county road because county personnel had negligently spread an excessive quantity of loose, angular gravel on the road during the preceding week, causing a hazardous condition. He wrote that Kamar slipped in the loose gravel while being ridden at a normal walking pace on the road and fell to his knees. He stated that Kamar's knees were seriously injured by the large, angular pieces of gravel and that it is uncertain whether Kamar will recover sufficiently to be ridden in the future. He added that I have incurred significant costs for Kamar's veterinary care. Trent, my vet, wrote a letter to the Santo County also. He explained how the carpal joints, overlying tissues and tendons crossing the joints on both front legs are extensively damaged and that Kamar may have permanent lameness from this injury. He mentioned that this event has been extremely time-consuming for me and that I have acquired significant expense. I am feeling so thankful that my lawyer and my vet are standing up for my case."

"This is all good news. I am glad to see you looking more cheerful. You were starting to worry me. You are getting so thin. You look worn to a shadow."

"I know. I have also started seeing Pearce again. I love Pearce but I am aware that a layer of animosity lies beneath his smiles."

"Are you still seeing your therapist?"

"Yes, I saw her recently, in fact. She always astounds me with the things I learn from her. In my last session, she helped me realize that I have had a lot of damaged men in my lifetime. I cannot help all the men I know from drowning. I need to be saved from drowning. I inherited the damaged masculine image from my father. This damaged masculine image was given to me at birth. I didn't create this pain. It is not my fault that I didn't get what I needed from my biological father. He was missing so I project a fantasy on to every man I meet. My problems are rooted in me trying to resurrect my father in every man I meet.

Kamar carries the image of the damaged masculine now. I am sticking with Kamar, trying to save his life because I cannot live without the image of healing the injured masculine. My life's work has been to heal the damaged masculine. Every man I have ever known has been crippled or wounded in some way and I have tried to heal each one of them. I need to stop giving my feminine to the debilitated man. I need to start healing the masculine inside of me.

JJ is hideously devitalized. Pearce was seriously wasted when I first met him. I healed Pearce in some deep ways. Now Pearce carries some genuine, healthy masculine energy. But I cannot depend on depleted men anymore. I need to save myself. I need to try and strengthen the weakest parts of myself. I am the only one who can make a difference in my life. I am saying 'good-bye' to all the damaged men in my life. I am not letting a man into my life that hurts me anymore. I need to say 'I see you for your dangerous self and unless you give me wisdom to help me, you cannot have me.' I don't want a man to have power over me now.

Both my mother and I have been extremely disappointed by weak, ill men. My mother and I are both trying to heal the damaged male image we carry inside us. We don't need to be hurt anymore. And guess what? The stronger I am with my inner masculine image, the more it will help Kamar heal!"

"Wow, Toni. This is incredible. Do you remember Goddess Isis of Egypt? Isis knew how not to give herself away for nothing. Isis demanded wisdom. Isis was devoted to the masculine inside her. The work of Isis is to go around and find the pieces of the broken male and bring all the pieces together. This is soul work. You are doing the work of Isis. All the male images you have are corrupt but salvageable. Well, maybe not JJ. He gives with one hand and takes with the other. I am glad to hear that you are giving up trying to heal truly dangerous men like him. Start to regenerate yourself as you are trying to regenerate the basic tissue of Kamar's joints and ligaments!"

⁂

Rosa is my psychic friend. She smokes cigarettes constantly and tells me she smokes to feel grounded to Mother Earth. Her curly black hair floats around her pale white face. She always wears vivid red lipstick. She is a large woman and wears big colorful dresses and leather sandals. She is very solemn. I rarely see her smile or laugh. It must be difficult to live on a mental platform, seeing and feeling everyone's energy.

"My vet is amazed at how quickly Kamar's knees are healing, Rosa. His knees are scabbed over so I don't have to bandage them anymore. His wounds are ninety-five percent closed. He is ready for me to start doing rehabilitation exercises for him. I plan to gently bend and straighten his knees every day. I will try to get some mobility in the knee joints. But the vet still warns me that Kamar may never walk again."

"Kamar is a pure soul, Toni. He deserves to live. I see Kamar healed and I see you riding Kamar again in a year."

"Really? Oh, this would be a miracle!" I am overjoyed! Will my prayers be answered?

"I also see a very immature and threatening man in your life. He pretends to love you but his love consists of 'I want.' He expects you to meet his insatiable need for emotional satisfaction. He does not permit you to be yourself but demands that you conform to his ideals and fulfill all his desires. He sees you as a counterpart of his selfish, needy personality. You need to say 'No' to him, Toni. This is the only way he can grow up. Instead of demanding satisfaction from you, he needs to recognize your individuality. Stop giving in to his hostile demands and live true to your own emotions. When you are no longer indulging childish men, you can be one-in-yourself, dependent on no man and a daughter of the Moon Goddess.

Metaphorically, the moon represents the inspiration and wisdom of nature. Rational thinking is sun mind. Moon mind is not academic thinking. Moon thinking is the motion of unorganized, unknown ideas that flow within your mind naturally. Learn to know your own depths and limits with your moon mind. Embrace a larger outlook on your life."

I understand what Rosa is saying to me. I know the immature man she is referring to is JJ. I have been fulfilling JJ's childish demands and he has turned into a callous, hard-hearted tyrant. I have to finally say 'No' to him. I will no longer give him what he wants. Now he will hopefully leave me alone and satisfy his needs somewhere else. I am glad that Rosa can see this.

"Rosa, can you clear away this man's harmful energy from my life?"

"This harmful man is possessed by evil spirits who feed off fear. You need to ground yourself to the earth while putting light around the crown of your head. This prevents you from feeding his demons your fear. You are more powerful than his demons, Toni. This man threatens to hurt you but his soul is feeble. He is on a windy, downward road with his drugs and alcohol to his own destruction. I am going to put a guardian angel named Sarah around you. She will protect you for the next six months. And I now disconnect your karma from this man."

Rosa makes huge slicing motions with her arms as she walks around me. I want JJ's pull on me to become weaker and weaker. I won't let him feed off my fear anymore. I will try not to talk about him anymore to anyone. I won't put energy into his name. I believe that spirituality begins with the body and with Mother Earth. As JJ's connections are severed from my aura, I feel my bond with the Earth and Moon Mother getting stronger inside me. I feel centered within myself.

"I would like to meet a mature man who isn't fragmented and wounded and who is capable of seeing me for who I am."

"Toni, keep working to eradicate your fear and apprehension. These emotions put holes in your energy field. Pray every day. Talk quietly. Stay calm. Trust in the Divine. Internalize the power of the Goddess."

∾

Kamar's right leg is very swollen and crippled. Whenever I take Silvano out for a ride, Kamar starts to buck and rear. He doesn't like being left behind in the corral. He gets excited and tries to run. Joy thinks his inclination to run is good. I love Kamar's desire to run. But he cannot walk at all at night. I have noticed the cold fall weather is making Kamar's knees stiff and painful.

I drive my little truck to Villa Vet to look at Kamar's X-rays.

"Look here, Toni. Kamar has bone spurs and arthritis starting to develop in his right knee. Kamar will always be lame. I know my prognosis is grim but I have to tell you what I see in the X-ray," Trent tells me without emotion.

I burst into tears. "I will do whatever it takes to heal Kamar. I will continue doing rehabilitation stretches, massage, water massage and magnet wraps. I will fatten him up with corn, corn oil and alfalfa pellets. I will get a wall feeder so Kamar doesn't hit his knees on the metal trough," I say, between sobs.

"I am the bad guy because I always make you cry."

"You are not the bad guy. I just don't want to give up. I love Kamar deeply. I get the most discouraged at night. Kamar's head is low to the ground and he cannot move." I cannot tell Trent that every day I pray to the Goddess, Mother of all Creation. I pray that Rosa's prediction that Kamar will be walking without pain in a year comes true.

"Did I tell you that my lawyer informed me that I lost my case with the Santo County? My lawyer tells me to cut my losses. I have already spent three thousand dollars trying to heal Kamar."

"I really hate to say this but you could have bought another purebred Arabian horse for this kind of money. I am going to ask you to give Kamar two more weeks. If Kamar continues to get worse, especially at night, I think he will need euthanasia."

"No. Kamar needs a chance. My mother tells me Kamar needs six months to get better. My friend Thomas recommends that I try acupuncture. I found an acupuncturist in Santo and he is coming out on Monday for Kamar's first appointment. I am not going to give up. Kamar must get better!"

"I admire your tenacity. Okay. Here is another suggestion. Please shorten Kamar's corral so he can't try to run around. Every time Kamar puts excessive weight on his knees when he bucks and rears, he is hurting himself. He cannot heal when he has too much pressure on his torn knees. His knees need rest and restraint to heal."

"Yes, I can get Brant to help me do this today."

&

Dr. May specializes in Japanese acupuncture and bodywork. He is stocky with blonde hair and a long brown mustache leaning from his mouth. He wears a loose-fitting white cotton shirt and slacks with sandals. I can tell that he has never spent time around a corral but he is warm-hearted and helpful. He takes one look at Kamar's swollen and crippled front knees and he gasps.

"I admit that I have never had a horse as a patient. I am willing to work with your horse but I can see that your horse needs a lot of care."

"I appreciate your kindness in coming to my ranch to work with Kamar. My friend Jane thinks it is my responsibility to put Kamar down as he is obviously miserable and in pain. Kamar's vet also recommends that he put Kamar to sleep. Other friends tell me that I should drive Kamar to a horse clinic in Colorado. My mother believes that Kamar will die in a week if he is taken off his current healthy diet that includes carrot pulp and supplements or if he is taken away from the best daily care and attention that I am giving him. I am giving his knees mustard and flour poultices, DMSO sweat wraps, magnet wraps, ultrasound treatments, infrared blanket wraps and liniments with goldenseal powder on his gashes. I am keeping a daily diary of all that I do and how Kamar reacts. I need to do what works until Kamar gets better. I don't know what works yet. But you have been highly recommended to me."

"Well, I hope I can help you. I know how negative people can be, especially vets, regarding alternative healing."

"You are right. I read a book on horses written by a vet and this vet claims that alternative therapy is a placebo and a fraud. Vets are scientific. They have zero faith."

"Acupuncture has been used for thousands of years in traditional Oriental medicine to enhance blood circulation, balance the nervous system and promote the release of pain-relieving hormones. It is a holistic approach that pin-points the problems individually. I can insert my metallic needles into specific meridian acupoints on Kamar's legs and back that will help bring down the swelling as well as promote healing."

"As you can see, Kamar is very crippled in his right knee. When he tries to walk, he drags his right leg. His left knee is still bleeding a combination of blood and joint fluid and I have to bandage it every day. I have been giving Kamar painkillers every day since the accident. I feel he has become a drug addict. I need you to help me bring down the swelling in both knees, promote healing in his bleeding knee and see if the acupuncture relieves his pain so I can get him off the drugs."

"From what you are telling me, I think the first thing we need to do is to stop giving Kamar the drugs. When you give him painkillers, Kamar feels no pain so he tries to walk. His wounds open up from movement and the swelling never has a chance to go down. Because the drugs mask the pain, Kamar is making himself worse. Let Kamar be in pain for a while so he stops moving around. Then he will rest his knees so they can have a chance to get better. Let's take him off the painkillers today.

I am also going to teach you massage techniques to get circulation into Kamar's knees. You will massage above and below the knee joints with emu oil. You can also start putting ice packs alternating with heating pads on Kamar's knees every day. Let me measure Kamar's knees now."

Dr. May takes out his measuring tape and stretches it gently around Kamar's swollen right knee. It is 12 3/4 inches. Kamar's left knee is 11 inches around. Then he takes out his acupuncture needles and taps them into various spots around Kamar's upper legs and back. I am surprised at how still Kamar stands for the treatment.

"Remember, Toni, Kamar will feel better after these treatments. He will want to jump around. Jumping will hurt him. Try to keep him quiet. Keep Kamar off the drugs so his pain forces him to keep weight off his knees. He needs to stand still. He needs to rest and heal. In time, he will be better without the drugs. The drugs are what are preventing Kamar from further improvement. If Kamar gets cranky without the drugs, you can give him an herb called valerian to calm him down."

"I am praying every day that I can get Kamar's knees to normal so he can live a long life!"

"I sincerely believe that humans are not superior to animals. We are all equal. Animals and plants are projections of ourselves: if we take care of plants and animals, this shows us how we are taking care of ourselves. We need to have compassion for our fellow creatures. It is the process of life that we honor, not necessarily the end result. After every process, there is another process. It is your karma, Toni, to learn how to heal Kamar."

"I don't mind this process. I just pray that the end result is that Kamar is running without pain and that I can ride him again!"

"With your determination and enthusiasm, I believe Kamar will be fine in a year."

"I am praying I can heal Kamar. I recently found out from my lawyer that everyone living on my road is making a petition to Santo County against the chipped gravel the County dumped on the road the day before my accident with Kamar. The gravel is what caused Kamar to fall. Many of my neighbors have had car accidents from slipping and sliding on the gravel. My lawyer says the law looks at my horse as if it was an object, like a car. My lawyer admits to me that he is a Taoist. He believes that animals have souls, unlike cars or objects. Isn't he a great lawyer?"

"What an unusual lawyer. You can create miracles, Toni. I will help you."

❧

Every time I walk Kamar around, he gets lame. He is not ready to walk. I measured his right knee today and it went from 12 3/4 inches to 12 1/2 inches. I measure his knees every day to see if the inflammation is going down. If the knees are inflamed, I do a sweat wrap.

I have a daily routine now. First, I grind up Kamar's supplements in a coffee grinder. His supplements include MSM, Arnica, birch, bromelain, Ruta Grava, microhydrin, spirilina, glucosamine and Rhus Tox. I feed Kamar his supplements with a cup of bran, corn oil and applesauce. Then I put ice packs on each knee for fifteen minutes. I do hand massage, stroking from his knees up to his shoulders as well as thumbing around the knees in a spiral to the center of the knees. I do water massage next for twenty minutes on each knee. I dry off his knees and do ultrasound on each knee for five minutes. I have learned that doing ultrasound over seven minutes cripples Kamar.

Dr. May taught me to insert the acupuncture needles myself because Kamar tried to kick him last week. Dr. May wrenched his back and he doesn't want to hurt himself again. So now I put acupuncture needles into Kamar's knees and back.

My mother advises me to apply heat on Kamar's knees. I put heat packs and hot poultices on his knees. Then I bandage each knee with magnets and infrared blankets. At night, I put thermowraps on his knees. Often, his knees are straighter after wearing them.

Kamar has been biting me lately. He wants more attention since he cannot walk. He needs his head and mouth to be handled. When he tries to bite me, I grab his nose between my hands and rub and rub until he tries to pull away from me.

Watching Kamar drag his right leg around is more than I can bear. This healing process is so up and down. Kamar seems better some days and then he is worse again. He has good days and bad days. I am trying to prolong his good days.

Some people I know act like there is something wrong with me for taking care of an injured horse. Vets keep telling me that Kamar's knees are chronic and won't be healed. All the vets who look at Kamar's X-rays tell me that there is nothing science can do to help heal his knees. They tell me that if I keep Kamar alive, he will never walk again. Horse people I know tell me I am selfish to keep Kamar alive. They say I need to hurry up, get my head together, do the humane thing and put Kamar down.

I don't like the obsessively human-focused society I live in. People seem so anxious and embarrassed by their vices. I want to avoid these people. I have met veterinarians that think of animals as money to be made. Some cowboys have no spiritual connection to nature. Most people I have met don't see the soul of the horse. To me, Kamar is a creature of the Divine. He enchants me. I need enchantment. Animals enchant me and always have. I am so glad when I get to be around animals all day.

My mother never betrays me like most people. Her gentle, thoughtful conversation and daily encouragement is teaching me about real love. Every day that Kamar seems worse, she tells me not to give up hope. She reminds me that she has healed herself of chronic ailments naturally and that I have a handicapped horse that needs nature and time to heal.

Since Kamar is especially crippled on cold days, I would like to live in a place that is warm in the winter so he can walk easier. My dream is to ride Kamar wherever I want for miles and miles in the desert. I have faith and I won't give up faith. I want all my good actions to produce a wondrous result.

☙

"I am so worried about you, Khalifah. You are twenty-nine-years old now. You look so unhappy. The only thing that excites you is your little daughter, Saida. I know you love her. But you can't chew food and you can't walk around. I can't let you starve to death. I love you so much, my sweet stallion. You have never once bucked me off. You have never kicked or reared. You don't bite. You are the best horse in the world. You are the most beautiful, loving and kind spirit of any being I have ever known. You are great. I will never forget you, ever. I will miss your stallion energy and vitality. But I don't want you to suffer. You look terrible. There is nothing more I can do to help you. I have to call Villa Vet and have a vet come and put you to sleep, my angel. I won't be able to watch this. I cannot. Mother told me she would be here with you.

I am going to cut off a piece of your mane and tail for a keepsake. I will try to be in prayer with a candle lit for you when the vet comes. I will bless you and surround you with love and light. I will visualize you in horse heaven."

I am weeping. Khalifah puts his nose by my head, moves his ears to listen to me and looks steadily at me with his big, brown eyes. Yes, he is the best horse I will ever ride. I can't help him physically anymore. I can only love him forever in the spirit world. I love my old horse and I only want what is best for him. Mother is right when she tells me that his condition will only get worse with time. I can't see him suffer. I am so sad that he has such an old body. I wish I could give him a new young body. Thank goodness I have many photographs to look at when I need to see him in all his youthful splendor. And I have all my happy memories.

"Good-bye, my old beloved Khalifah. I will talk to your spirit. I will listen to the tape recording I made of you whinnying for Saida. I will hold your piece of mane and tail and look at your photos. I cherish you. You are my beautiful old stallion."

Khalifah died at two in the afternoon. I was at Pearce's house, crying and crying, when Khalifah died. Mother called me after the truck took Khalifah away.

"He was very brave, Toni. He wasn't afraid of the vet. I fed him the carrot pulp you left for him. I caressed his forehead as he fell gently to the ground. It is all over."

Pearce holds me tightly as I thank my mother and hang up the phone. My sobs turn into moans and I gasp for breath.

"I feel dead. I feel lost. I just want Khalifah. Heaven doesn't look so bad. I just want to be with my old friend Khalifah," I say with utter despair.

"Little sweetie, I know how difficult and sad today is for you. It will take some time to get through all this grief, I'm sure. All I can say is I love you very much. I will call you every day and I know that each day will get better for you. We will never forget Khalifah."

"How will I survive without my sweet stallion in my life?"

"You will survive this sorrow, I promise."

"My mother knew how much I would need Kamar at the time of Khalifah's death."

"Yes, you have horses, cats, dogs and goats who need you."

"Thank you for reminding me. And thank you for giving me comfort."

ೲ

"Pearce, could you rub my sore hands? They hurt from all the daily massage I give Kamar's knees."

"No, I don't want to," he says frigidly.

"Why can't you give me what I need?"

"I cannot help you. I expect you to take care of yourself."

"I need your support."

"I cannot support you. I am broke. You need to make your own money. And I hate all the money you are still spending on Kamar."

"I am trying to make my own money. I wish I could make more." I know that my request for Pearce to massage my sore hands has nothing to do with money. Pearce criticizes me more and more, every chance he gets. He condemns me more when he is unhappy with his own life. I truly want Pearce to succeed at something so he feels good about himself. I love Pearce but I feel like he really doesn't care about me. He wants me to take care of him.

"I hate eating with your animals around."

"Why are you so mean to me?" I actually know the answer to my question. He is miserable. He is jealous of my life. He is jealous of my beauty and my talents. He covets my little ranch. I have started to teach yoga at a spa in Santo. I already have twenty-five people in every class I teach. Students love my classes. I am so happy I have found my niche. Pearce envies my happiness. He wants what I have.

"You need to obey me and follow my guidelines, Toni."

"Are you God?"

"Everyone knows that we were once good for each other but now I cannot handle the way you live your life."

"You used to talk about getting certified in teaching yoga with me. You wanted us to get jobs teaching yoga around the world. I thought you seriously wanted to rebuild our lives together. We both love yoga. I think you love studying Kriya Yoga as much as you love your guitar."

"I don't trust you anymore. I won't tolerate your behavior with other men."

"You are just jealous that men like me."

"I see no future for us anymore."

"Do you still love me, Pearce?"

"I hate it when you ask me if I love you."

"I need reassurance."

"I hate your insecurity."

"Why can't you say anything nice to me!" I am exasperated with him.

"I won't be prompted to say anything nice."

"I am the best thing that ever happened to you, Pearce."

"I'm stuck with you."

"You can be so cruel. I can't be around you when you are frustrated with your own life."

"I don't value your love anymore."

"It's me, your little sweetie, here in front of you."

"Don't touch me. Don't look at me or talk to me anymore."

"Why are you so gloomy? When your parents visited my ranch recently, they were impressed by my life and all the animals I take care of. I showed them the rehabilitation stretch therapy exercises I am doing on Kamar's front legs and they said they were very proud of me. I told them about all the daily supplements I give Kamar and they were astonished at the way I am healing Kamar naturally. Kamar is moving around more. Pearce, I really believe that someday I will be able to ride Kamar again. Isn't this amazing?"

"I don't want to rain on your parade," he says crossly.

"I think it is better if I stay away from you when you are so grumpy." I start to hate Pearce when he is ill-tempered. He kills any love I feel for him when he finds fault with me constantly. His cruelty towards me makes me angry. He doesn't appreciate me. My mother tells me I am beautiful when I am happy. Pearce doesn't value beautiful women. And when I am happy, Pearce gets sulky. I want to share my joy with him but he just wants to squash me like a bug. He can't manage my life anymore. He can't handle me or my decisions. He refuses to help me.

"You don't like the jazz music I play. You don't like being a musician's girlfriend. You don't like going to jazz concerts with me. And I don't like hammering nails or fixing fences. I don't like living in the country. I don't like hiking with your dogs or riding your horses. I don't feel comfortable at your house anymore as your mother knows I can't support you. I don't want to teach yoga with you. I'm not as good as you are doing yoga. We are incompatible, Toni. I know I am sexy and you only want my body. I don't want intense love anymore. I want a woman who has money. I want a woman who likes jazz and who likes to stay up all night with me. I need a woman who supports my life. You need a rancher who can load horses."

"You are using any excuse you can find to make me feel bad." Deep in my heart, I know that he is right about me finding another man. I need a man who takes pride in providing for his woman.

"I don't want to talk anymore. It only opens my wounds."

"I hear that you are spending time with Sheila. I know she still takes care of you and buys you expensive things like leather jackets and new guitars. I know you accepted lots of money from her to produce your new album. I used to envy her wealth. But she is buying you, Pearce. You are like a little boy who needs a rich mother. You are stuck with a cold woman with very little feminine healing power. With her, you will dry up. You will have very little creative and emotional strength without the life force and juice of the goddess of love and beauty, Goddess Aphrodite. You will be empty and sterile with Sheila.

I healed you, Pearce. When I met you, you were living in a bottle of wine every day and night. I resurrected you from your death wish. I gave you desire and sexual energy. Now you think you are better off without me but you will wither away."

I know that Pearce could never understand my femininity. I want powerful feminine potency in my life. I am so much more loving than he is. He thrived on my love once. He just doesn't have the ongoing capacity to love me. He has no business being with me when he has no desire to care for me. Pearce hates me for wanting him to be a man and feel responsible for me. He is used to women supporting him. He needs a financially secure woman that he doesn't envy who is normal and mediocre. Then he will feel better about himself.

I am not normal. I am natural. I am dedicated to the divine feminine, to the Goddess and to Mother Earth. As long as I have my animals around me, I am happy. I adore my animals. They make me feel loved. They complete me. And I am determined to ride Kamar again. He and I are growing to trust one another more and more.

I don't want to fight with Pearce anymore. Let him fly away from me. He is unhealthy for me now. His desire to take what I have, his mean streak and his controlling personality separated us. I loved Pearce's body and soul once. To me, he was my tall, slender, dark and handsome Adonis. I never wanted to give up his beauty.

Pearce left my life forever in April.

〰

It is the middle of May. Today is a big day for me. Bob, my new horse trainer, believes Kamar is ready for me to ride in the round pen. Bob gives me lots of assurance as well as solid technique.

"Kamar no longer needs to be lunged, Toni. This will only encourage him to be wild. Before you saddle Kamar, fling a rope up and around his body. Then, put a thin blanket on his back. Because you told me he doesn't like to be tied up, hold his halter rope around your left elbow while you put his saddle on. Always use a snaffle bit with Kamar. Once you are up in the saddle, look where you want Kamar to go. If you want him to go to the right, kick your right foot against his belly and look right. When Kamar moves right, stop kicking. Kick both your legs on his belly to get him to move forward. When he moves forward, stop kicking and rub his neck with long strokes from his ears to his withers. This will relax him. If Kamar wants to run away with you, grab the left rein with both hands to your left hipbone. Let the right rein be loose. Don't let go until Kamar stops turning in circles and drops his head. Then release the reins and rub his neck from ears to withers.

After each ride, tie Kamar to a tree for thirty minutes with the saddle on to teach him that it is more fun to be ridden than to stand around feeling bored. I think Kamar is a smart horse. He learns fast. I like him. You will be great together."

Brant walks up to the round pen with his camera. As I get on Kamar for the first time since his accident ten months ago, I am elated! I am smiling so much my cheeks hurt! Brant takes lots of photos. I don't ever want to forget this day. I can ride Kamar again! I have been praying for months for this day. My happiness is my reward for all the dedicated work and devoted effort I put into Kamar's recovery. Kamar is lively. I can tell he is glad to be able to walk again. The fact that I am riding him when all the vets claimed he would never walk again and that I would never ride him again is astounding. Yes, miracles happen!

"Tell Bob how the vets at Villa Vet refer people with injured horses to you now, Toni," Brant says proudly.

I stop Kamar and ask him to stand quietly.

"Yes, it is pretty amazing when a person calls me and asks my advice regarding a seriously injured horse. I tell each horse owner that if he or she can answer 'yes' to five questions, then the horse owner needs to do whatever it takes to keep the horse alive."

"What are the five questions?" Bob asks with interest.

"Question number one is 'Do you have money?' It takes an abundance of money for vet bills and alternative healing methods to keep a horse alive. I am lucky as my sweet mother gave me her credit card and told me I didn't need to pay her back until I had a good job down the road.

Question number two is 'Do you have time?' It takes many hours a day to clean and bandage a horse's wounds. It takes lots of time to undertake all the healing methods necessary. Healing Kamar was a full-time job for me.

Question number three is 'Do you have emotional support?' You will need a person who is your emotional rock. When things look grim, this person encourages you and reassures you that things will get better, in time. I have my mother. She believes in the natural healing properties of Mother Nature. She always reminded me not to listen to the negative vets or gloomy friends who told me to put Kamar down. She always listens when I sob in despair or doubt. She always comforts me with her hugs and her words of praise and hope. I could not have done this without my loving mother.

Question number four is 'Do you love your horse?' I love Kamar so deeply. He is a gift to me from my mother. He is my little gray horse and my source of great pleasure and visual delight!

Question number five is 'Does your horse want to live?' Kamar could have given up, laid down and died. He didn't. Throughout the ten months I struggled to heal his knees, his ears were forward, his eyes were clear and he had a strong will to live. Never once did Kamar give up. Kamar is a hardy and tough Arabian horse. His courage to get better reinforced my hope and desire that he would improve a little each day."

"Why did you give your horse the name he has?" Bob asks with a smile. Bob is a cowboy and I doubt he has ever heard the word 'Kamar' before.

"Well, 'Kamar' is Arabic for 'the moon.' Arabian horses often turn white as they age. My stallion Khalifah was gray when I got him as a yearling. By the time Khalifah was twenty-years-old, he was pure white. Kamar is gray with a black mane and tail. Now, he is like the New Moon.

As he gets older, Kamar will be turning white like the Full Moon. I want Kamar to live a long life! And I plan to be riding him for twenty more years!"

What I cannot say aloud to Brant or Bob is that the moon has esoteric meaning for me. I love to study ancient civilizations. One primitive story is that the moon is a man who appears as a waxing crescent and he fights the darkness represented by a dragon. The moon is triumphant and comes to his fullness as a wise and great king on earth. This moon god is a woman's guardian and protector. He is the permanent husband and fertilizing presence of a woman. The marriage of man and woman is of no account. The true husband is the moon. The moon is called Lord of Women.

Marriage to the moon makes a woman one-in-herself. Her strength is in herself. Her strength lies in being herself. She dares to listen to inspiration from within. She contacts the deeper part of her own nature. She has the wisdom of nature that knows without knowing why.

The moon is the ruler of the night and the unconscious which controls the mysterious forces beyond human understanding. A woman is ruled by these inner laws. A woman wants to be by herself at times so she can withdraw from the demands of the external world. She craves to live in the secret places of her heart. She has a wild aspect to her nature. She yearns to keep animals close to her. She looks for renewal and spiritual awakening which lies within her.

The moon represents rebirth of hope, the possibility of transcending the past and the ability to start again, even after disaster and failure. After all the traumatic distress I have endured this last year, I feel that now I can start again with new values and new understanding. As my mother promised me throughout Kamar's healing process, life renews itself again and again. I ask myself 'What does it mean?' It means that I am experiencing my inner voice and I am allowing it to speak to learn my depths and limits. Going to the abyss as I have is an initiation. Experiences of initiation produce feelings of supreme awareness.

My moon horse, Kamar, has been given a new chance at life. He is an inspiration to me. He shows me the significance of listening to nature to renew life. Like the life of the moon, I can partake in a new chance at life with Kamar. I have found deep instinct and passion of my own. I have converted my energy into achieving the valuable work of saving the life of my beloved, young horse. I have a role to play that is my own. I do what I do not because of any desire to please, not to be liked or to be praised and not because of any need to gain power over another. I am not dependent on what other people think. What I do is true to myself. I say 'No' when it would be easier to say 'Yes.' I cannot be possessed or owned. I belong to myself. I take risks. I do the hardest thing on earth for myself. Other people say it can't be done but I am the person doing it.

CPSIA information can be obtained
at www.ICGtesting.com
Printed in the USA
LVHW040607060922
727610LV00006B/440